WISE

&

OTHERWISE

JOSHUA SCOTT

outskirtspress
DENVER, COLORADO

Outskirts Press, Inc.
http://www.outskirtspress.com

ISBN: 978-1-4787-4288-3

Library of Congress Control Number: 2014915212

Outskirts Press and the "OP" logo are trademarks belonging to Outskirts Press, Inc.

PRINTED IN THE UNITED STATES OF AMERICA

WELCOME TO THE JUNGLE

I arrived at the 14th floor of this "wanna-be" high-rise building in the heart of the commercial district. The elevator that brought me up to the top floor was a sign of the times: glittery, provocatively ornate, and fast on the move. It was the mid-'80s, the go-go years of the millennia. An era of shifting loyalties, of deceitful truces and hidden rivalries, of pirate-businessmen begging for respectability through their newly acquired wealth, and of decent people hanging on to the shreds of their family names and their family's silver.

I was 22, freshly graduated, and as covetous and resolute for power as *Brute* on the eve of his show of parental affection. All my self-control skills and my mental focus were in high gear and nothing, let alone anyone, was going to stop me from making a lasting impression at today's meeting. Before reaching the terminus of this elevated journey, I accomplished the anxious man's trilogy: I combed my hair with both my hands, holding my head for a split second as if to keep all my ideas in place; then, I tucked my shirt in my underpants, entrusting to their rubber endings what my laundry lady could never get straight, and finally I adjusted my tie, which looked even more twisted than before my "let's-look- sharp" move. Destiny, here I come.

The elevators door opened on a V-shaped mahogany desk harboring a 50-something stiff-necked "executive assistant" (the politically correct term for a secretary in these feminist revival days!). She was keeping busy while sipping iced coffee and spitting bullets into the intercom. I reckoned that the being behind the human mask was very familiar, albeit unfriendly. In a Proust-like moment, her face reminded me of scenes from horror movies. Think Frau Blucher in Mel Brooks' *Young Frankenstein*. That kind of overpaid help (that's what I would give her as correct appellation), lives in corporate settings from Rome to Rio as if cloned by some deranged genetic scientist. And they multiply.

I recalled what my mother had instructed me when dealing with non-principals on first encounters. "Be politely cold but not warm," she said, "for warmth in high spheres is equated with weakness. Look in the direction of the person you are addressing, but not at them, for such a show of interest will elevate them to your status and thus, diminish the moral barrier you must erect." Finally, "You should not ask for the person you are about to meet, but rather say: Mr. So-and-so requested to see me (a sign of self-importance); I trust I am on time (a show of business etiquette); please inform him of my presence (a conclusion by a direct order through the deceitful use of the word 'please')." Quite a piece of motherly advice, don't you agree?

"Hello, I am expected by Mrs. Gotryne; please announce me at once." Granted, my altered version of the perfect encounter with-the-lesser-kind was more dramatic than my mom's instructions. But then, I have already warned you about my feisty personality.

Ms. Hard Nose (as I intend to refer to the executive assistant) was obviously unimpressed by my performance. She killed a few seconds before addressing me with her morbid voice: "And who shall I announce, please?" replied the receptionist (enough niceties about her job description and let's call a spade a spade).

"She would know, because I am expected."

"Don't be so sure," countered the insolent one.

Finally, striking back at the evil vampire, I replied that I was "crystal clear on that, ma'am." I think the combination of my street vendor voice and the deliberate use of the senior-citizen connotation in "ma'am" worked beautifully on Ms. Tightlipped a.k.a. Hard Nose (just a name alternation for those of you who are already confused at the beginning of this story, and you may be quite a few). After an exchange on the intercom with Mrs. Gotryne's secretary, the receptionist's grin melted like an ice cube in the Mojave Desert. I was escorted into a private living room and politely asked to wait for Mrs. Gotryne.

The room was painted in shades of hunter green and framed with equestrian prints of British champions, all traceable to the great Godolphin & Darley Arabian. The fake antique furniture betrayed the need of all newly established financial institutions to be modeled after the Rothschilds or Warburgs, or seriously risk being mistaken for a financial supermarket (no offense intended to American Express, Sears Roebuck, or the Travelers Group). The old-world decor was brought back to our century by copies of the FT laid on the coffee table. A Reuters screen in the right corner was showing market quotes from Europe. At 11:00 a.m. local time, only the European markets were active, and the few awakened Wall Street traders were busy celebrating the bull market in some shady after-hours club on Manhattan's lower East Side.

I was about to meet Mrs. Gotryne, the General Secretary of Inter-Finance, a financial conglomerate with business spanning from banking to oil and gas, and almost everything in between. Inter-Finance was involved in shipbuilding in Korea, chemicals in Basle, printing and publishing in Germany, construction materials in Italy, wineries and labeled perfume in France, and mining concessions in Africa. Not to mention financial services in NY.

Mrs. Gotryne was a close family friend. Some filthy minds insisted that she was too close a family friend--more precisely, a conquest of my late father's. Gossip aside, Mrs. Gotryne was Inter-Finance's Eminence Grise, its CEO's top confidante. Whether my late father wandered into the silk stockings of that lady was not one of my immediate concerns. Blame it again on my greedy character for not having held my father accountable on a post-mortem basis for all his extra-marital escapades, and instead exploiting them as the very ropes of my corporate climbing. So what? Sue me!

Soraya, Mrs. Gotryne's secretary came to escort me into her boss' office. Soraya was a cross between a purebred Arabian mare and an African panther: in short, a breathtaking and deadly combination. "Mrs. Gotryne will see you now, if you'd like to follow me." *I'd follow you right to the last stop of my life's train,* was my unuttered reply. However, my senses back, I offered nothing in the form of an answer except an uncomfortable smile. Soraya was a brunette with blonde (and blunt) ambitions--a definition I will attempt to fully elaborate on, but later. For now she was my guiding light into the dark corridors of this corporate tunnel, and I was a delighted tour guest.

I was escorted into Nadia's office, where she was sitting behind a black marble-topped desk with tens of documents piled up. "You have your dad's eyes," said Nadia with an authoritarian tone mixed with a touch of angst. Nadia had not seen me since Dad passed away. She quickly proceeded to explain why I was summoned to her office today. Inter-Finance, as the spiel went on, was in full expansion mode and on the lookout for new talents to assume mid-level positions. There was a Manchurian system for recruiting hand-picked senior personnel in anticipation of succession planning. To be more precise, she stated that Inter-Finance was looking for one more candidate to add to its stable of corporate studs. Who was to question this self-serving recruiting policy? Not the young and thirsty me. Was my wildest dream coming true? An invitation to join the big leagues by skipping the rubbish of the minor leagues' mandatory passage…leapfrogging all that time in the saddle that you're expected to endure before landing a job at the likes of Inter-Finance? This was no ordinary job offer. Calling it a lifetime opportunity would be more appropriate.

Nadia did not beat around the bush. "Your academic record is solid, your IQ test results were within the upper ranges, and your family background is highly desirable." Did she mean that literally, having first-hand evidence/feel of the matter? "Your social behavior is rather decent." Rather decent! What in the name of God did she mean by that? Had these devils run a check on me? Did they know secrets of my social life? My forays into raunchy circles, including my ongoing affair with a married lady (though with a distasteful second-rate husband); or my addiction to uppers, a legacy of my college days?

"Sam," she said, calling me back from my confused introspection, "all of the above features are quite available in many young men in town." What made me special to her, as she explained, was the fact that she could personally vouch for my loyalty and social fabric. Nadia's last statements left me with no illusion regarding to whom I would eternally owe my entry at Inter-Finance: Nadia Gotryne. The woman, who loved the Father, aided the Son and eventually conspired with the Holy Ghost.

From what I gathered, my job description was rather simple. My title would be that of Assistant Vice President for Corporate Affairs. My role was to encompass general corporate and administrative matters, including the review of all memoranda addressed to or from Nadia, taking the minutes of the Board of Directors, coordinating contacts with foreign counsels and advisers, and handling of certain files deemed too sensitive for general staff. My office was a sign of my relative unimportance, being located on the 5th floor, not on the all-powerful top 14th floor. My salary, the core interest for self-declared greedy bastards like me (and we are plenty in this world, so please wipe out this stupid, outraged, socialist, save-the- dolphins grin from your face) was $5000 a month in addition to many perquisites. I wanted to shout out a "Yes" that would shatter the glass of the Twin Towers and create havoc for weeks on end. On second thought, I wanted call my classmates and rub their noses in my startling success. My other idea--the most absurd of them all, if you can imagine (if you have gotten this far in reading my pages, I know you have that capacity) was to ask Nadia for some time to think about it. But providence prevented me from this mortal sin, from looking a gift horse in the mouth on the very same day it returned from a full vet check.

Nadia's voice brought me back to reality like a trumpet to the wandering legions. It was sharp but yet comforting: "We'll settle it right away; no need for delays on this, right?" On that memorable day I thought that lady luck not only smiled at me, but also was taken by a hysterical laughter. Nadia buzzed in her lady in waiting, the sensual Soraya, to bring us coffee, and one of the special red contracts. Soraya obliged with grace while avoiding eye contact with me at any cost, as if to assure her boss that my charm never even came close to touching her.

Signing a contract without first reviewing it is firmly not within my habits. For a layperson it is a grave mistake. For a man of the law it is a crime. The contract before me had more confidentiality clauses than a Swiss banking account. I was the second party to the agreement and Triangle Star was the first party. Excuse my laborious mind, but Triangle Star was an unknown entity to me. I ventured a polite question on the issue.

"Who is Triangle Star?" I dared ask.

"That is none of your immediate concern," replied Nadia.

I was faced with a serious dilemma. Should I read the contract at my leisure, which could consume several hours, because of the anal-retentive attitude that I had developed toward the written word? That in theory was the right thing to do. Or should I skip all the legal mumbo-jumbo and affix my full signature on the dotted line? Doing that would be obeying the first order of my benefactor, though compromising my professional training and violating my scarce rules of self-discipline.

I smiled, looked at Nadia's brown eyes, and without looking any further for ands, ifs, or royal butts, I put my signature where it belonged. At that moment I knew deep inside that a small crack in my inner walls had appeared. A strange feeling of bitter joy filled my heart. My eyes, the mirrors of the soul as a great man once said, reflected the contrast of a bursting happiness and contained sorrow. As if the water in my eyes debated whether to glow with a joyous shine or to rain with tears, it stopped short of both, but crystallized and froze my vision for a while.

Back to business: I was to report as early as next morning at 7:30 a.m. Soraya escorted me to the elevator with such an improvised indifference that I had to retain myself from asking her to relax and at least to look where she was heading to avoid bumping into the sharp corners of the corridors on our way to the elevator. I headed back home, took a long bath, had a short nap prior to embarking on my nightly cruise in celebration.

Sobering up seven months later, I simply hated my job. I had wished so hard for it that I was devastated by the clerical tasks I was enduring. Proofreading! Never in my wildest dreams did I ever imagine myself armed with a pen and a ruler, combing interminable documents in search of grammatical errors. This was a Strunk and E.B. White's haven, not mine. You might think this was a tempest in a teacup, but nothing could be further from the truth. I always distrusted those who insisted that in order to see the big picture you ought to acquaint yourself with trivial pursuits. Hogwash, I say. Call it intellectual elitism, snobbery, or some other derogatory term that crosses your mind. I was not to subject my mental faculties to such menial jobs. No person with the slightest aspiration would voluntarily acquiesce to mediocre tasks. I am not being repetitive, only persistent. Those who assert that chores form personalities haven't had one to start with.

It may finesse your talents in discovering new and increasingly absurd tricks to kill time, like the double-action slingshot I had conceived of thick rubber and paper clips. It may even deepen your knowledge of your anatomy when exploring the wonders of skin moles, of soap crust that find refuge in your ears right after your daily shaving experience, or the joys of excavating your nostrils with pens, pencils, and other sharp instruments. But form a personality, never!

The bread and butter of my office was answering inquiries on the progress of my review (proofreading, for the uninitiated) of voluminous business documents. I recall Disraeli saying that with words do we govern people, but he must have overlooked the labor it entails to produce the correct word these days. Hours of proofreading, Mr. Disraeli! Enough hours to make you relinquish any joys or privileges of governing. However, I must admit that I had a fair share of spare time on my hands, which I assiduously used to strengthen my grip over my wonderful office operatives.

First was my male secretary, Rami Tarrab, a discreet, well-dressed gay gentleman. His sexual orientations were no concerns of mine, though they have incensed many on our floor. I really do not understand the anger of non-homophobes toward gay people. Do they fear conversion to the cause? I never figured that one out. My explicit support of Rami's way of life provided me with the edge I was looking for. In exchange for my approbation of his "situation," as it was called at that time, I was to enjoy his undivided loyalty. It is not true that homosexuals are a girl's best friends. Diamonds maybe, or me for a qualitative change. I instilled in Rami a trust that was unparalleled. I used to tell him that if anyone called in my absence, looking for me, he was to deny knowledge of my whereabouts, at any cost. Although he himself would not know where I was at the time, he nonetheless felt that we were sharing a secret denied to the general public. By way of deception was the marching order of my office.

We also agreed on a distinct filing code for documents and sensitive files. The 5th floor--and any floor, for that matter, except the almighty 14th--was considered enemy territory. Trust only yourself, Nadia had endlessly repeated. All routine memoranda were labeled "Personal: Aunt Huguette." Aunt Huguette was a dull, unassuming relative of mine whom I loathed because of her iguana breath and her outrageous outfits. She made the Queen of the Brits look like CoCo Chanel by comparison. Huguette was a fixture at all our family gatherings. She would come before the genuine guests, eat first, fall asleep last, and burden me with the undesirable task of escorting her back to her apartment. She had a conversational repertoire that focused on her little boy (he was forty-five at that time) and who had been studying medicine for the past twenty years of his adult life--if he had experienced any, that is. Her William was in Paris. His studies were remarkable, she used to say; he sends all his love, and is looking forward to visiting us in the summer. Little did she know that William had changed his name to Alfredo, was living in Lugano, working as a hairdresser and married to a Finnish lady who hated the sight of anyone, including William.

Correspondence files relating to foreign counterparts were dubbed "Xenophobia." I thought that my subtle coding system was too brash till the day Soraya, visiting our floor on a rare occasion, pointed to my "Xenophobia" file cabinet and asked whether it was wise to keep my medical records lying around the office. The covert makeover of my files had worked! Just as Salvador Dali, when required by his authoritarian wife to paint the radiator box, obliged by painting on it a duplicate picture of a radiator. Is that what the experts call Absurd Art? My dull office life was either turning me into a great artist or an absurd thinker, a difference of little difference. Finally, internal mail between my office and Nadia's was called "Oedipus Letters" for the emotional ties that bound us.

I will spare you the reaction of my office mates when they use to hear me scream through the intercom: "Rami, is Aunt Hugette's stuff finally coming or does it need more time?" or "Did you sort out my Oedipus issue for the day and wrote the Xenophobic statements for international marketing?" My ability to shock my shallow fellow office mates was never fading or in want of scripts.

Then, came my messenger boy Hanna: short, dark-skinned and with a nasal protuberance equal only to Cyrano's. Besides his primitive look, Hanna was an efficient messenger. His eyes sparkled with unspoken guilt and dripped with street-smart chatter. I always figured that he belonged to a pack, not to a family. How could he? He never spoke of his loved ones, relatives, or even his life outside the walled universe of my office. I admire those self-effacing subordinates whose lives vanish at the sight of yours. Nothing mattered to Hanna. No war, no peace, or truce in between. Only my satisfaction was written in neon lights in the midst of his conspicuous conscious. My newspapers, foreign and local alike, were neatly arranged on the left-hand corner of my desk, my incoming mail positioned in the center of the table, my coffee fresh and steaming at 7:30 a.m., and Hanna's welcoming smile were my early-morning rituals. He was prompt in delivering messages and quick in gathering information and returning salutes. All his verbal exchanges were accompanied by circumstantial facial grins. "Ms. Soraya says hello" was always delivered with a macho smile. "Mr. Wazk would like a chat, if you don't mind" was delivered with a disgusted twist of the mouth to signal the unimportance of the matter. "I saw the chairman in Mrs. Gotryne's office" was offered with a wink and the tightening of the lower lip as if he had gained inside information. I liked Hanna and always greeted or scolded him with the same imperious tone. "Hanna," I used to say when I was satisfied with his services, "nobody can even measure with half of you." On other less pleasant occasions, I used to tell him that if I had ordered a busload of dumbasses and received only him, I would consider the order fulfilled. He looked at me with pious admiration. The Gospel according to Saint Me.

Despite the vivid imagination I had devised to fill the dullness of my office work, I was seriously frustrated, and a cloud tainted with dark colors was hovering over me. Boredom is a dangerous form of decay and lack of prospects is a fearsome state. Those who really believe that their destiny was shaped in their early twenties ended up joining the fire brigade, or became part-time school supervisors or enlisted in their dad's business to assume the role of preppy jerks they originally were destined to have.

Was this part of my training? Who designs these types of internships, the Marquis de Sade's grandchild? I was doing a job that could have been handled by any moron in the legal department with both hands tied behind his back. Or perhaps I wasn't made for the corporate world and its rigidity after all. This dreadful thought haunted me for a long time. But I wisely decided to accept a more paced existence and to quietly consume the poisonous liquid of daily routine with the joys of sipping a Romanée-Conti 1936. No time for complaining, second-guessing, or mind games. Back to work with a phony smile and a fake face. Faking being an important tool in one's life, I had to hone my skills in that art of false moods and deceit. We fake all the time. Actions and attitudes are not always the genuine reflections of reality. Sometimes, they are designed to deceive others but often to deceive us. Without slipping into the philosophical theme of "the benefits of faking" and tiring the decent souls of my readers, or even worse, insulting the few self-appointed intellectuals who bequeath upon us the privilege of glancing through this un-intellectual work, I would like to state that faking is a necessary subterfuge to attain a higher good. To put your skeptical minds at peace, think about faked orgasms. They do exist and more frequently then we like to admit. Men consider them an insult to their sexual prowess or lack thereof. I, to the contrary, see them as a generous and most essential contribution by the female gender to the unbridled male ego and our sometimes-failing stamina. Analyze this: it's difficult to live through a fake orgasm--if you ever discover it--but it's devastating to live without any. So I went faking my way through the dungeons of the corporate world hoping for a drastic change, and soon!

CASINO ROYALE

The luxury cars parked outside the office signaled a high-level meeting on the 14th floor. The chairman's Bentley was ominously blocking the entrance of the building, and his legion of bodyguards was scattered in every corner of the lobby. In third-world countries, the number of armed guards is not correlated with risk levels. It is rather connected to social status and the degree of wealth. The more you can afford, the merrier. The JFK assassination, and that of a half-dozen of US presidents before him, should be enough signs to humble any security expert who insist on "zero tolerance" for security breaches. So one guard or a hundred wouldn't make a difference, in my inexperienced opinion.

All the other cars were parked behind the Bentley in order of their owners' importance. The fat cats of management did not spare any expense in picking their modes of transportation. All had a ridiculous display of multiple antennas glued onto the car trunks, almost convincing the laymen that they were in the presence of a NSA mobile-tracking station. I had no clue about the reason behind this muscle-flexing show. A note on my desk simply summoned me to Nadia's office. There was nothing on the regular agenda. Not to my knowledge, that is. I told Rami to stay put and hurried up to the top floor. The air was thickened by cigar smoke and loud bickering. The chairman, Rutger Zarmat, was quietly observing half a dozen directors cut each other's throats and their respective rights, so to speak. He was mildly smiling, and somewhat detached, but definitely in control…because all of the rest were losing it.

I took the seat right behind Nadia and positioned my notebook on my lap, prepared to scribble some lines. Rutger Zarmat took off his gold-rimmed glasses and pressed his right arm across his forehead as if to indicate a sudden malaise. Gradually, silence fell in the boardroom and quiet replaced the Tower of Babel atmosphere.

Zarmat's voice was suave but filled with authority. "I have heard your positions gentlemen. I agree with most of them to a certain degree. Therefore, I suggest that we take a pause before we decide all issues at hand." I was later briefed that Inter-Finance's casino in Madeira was the main topic of this emergency meeting. The Spanish authorities were threatening to close it down on some vague legal grounds. The profits of the casino had been robust in the past three years. Apparently, the irregularities detected by the Spanish authorities were not directly related to the practices of the gaming outlet. Whatever were their origins, they had to be cleared to keep the casino's doors open and the cash machines afloat. A resolution had to be adopted to that effect.

A motion was put before the board by the chairman--to whom the directors gave unanimous consent--to appoint a task force headed by Cyrus Alai, an Iranian businessman and a close friend of the chairman, to review, assess, and assist the casino in its dire straits. From a procedural point of view, that was the wrong thing to do. Appointing an outsider to Inter-Finance, a non-corporate exec, to deal with the casino's regulators would be viewed as an awkward gesture and turn them hostile. I had no say in the matter, so I kept my mouth shut, which in itself was a commendable act of self-discipline. To my surprise, I was deputized by Inter-Finance to accompany Cyrus to an extended journey to the Costa del Sol to attend to this casino business. I naively assumed that my legal talents were so dear to Inter-Finance. A wild gamble, I figured, since we were talking casinos here.

No further business was put before the board, and the meeting was brought to an end. The chairman disappeared in a sea of armed guards and his entourage of lawyers. You could never tell who was more lethal, a bodyguard with a loaded machine gun, or a lawyer with a filled fountain pen. Betting being a newly acquired habit of mine, I would stake the farm on the lawyer any day. Nadia asked me to wait in her office. When I stepped in, Soraya was working at filing some documents. Do you have premonitions about physical encounters? I mean in a biblical way? Well, it happens to me. Not as frequently as I wish, because you can be sure that I have had my fair share of rejections. Longing for body heat, I often ended up with body blows and more than just a bruised ego. But Soraya was the fruit of that poisonous tree of lust. Adam had it so easy compared with the present successor of Eve. I would eat a watermelon from her hands, let alone a skinny apple. And Soraya, as you already suspect, read my mind vividly. She knew I was waiting for the slightest sign to come forward, and knew that delaying that moment would only prolong her pleasure and extend my agony. Smart girl.

"We never see you around," she said in a nonchalant voice. "Are you still with us, or have you quit already?" A catchy answer was my only chance to make a lasting impression.

"I will play hard to quit and you'll play hard to get, and we'll see who scores first."

She blushed. Soraya was not prepared to argue with me. She was testing the waters and found them steamy hot. She stood tall, staring me in the eyes as to hypnotize me, and then with a little effort, she blew wind in my face, opening her crimson red mouth. I leaned forward as to whisper something to her and gently kissed the lobe of her left ear. For a moment the earth moved under me. Soraya's perfume spread on her baby skin was an elixir for longevity and happiness.

Without any brisk movements and in total control of her senses (and mine) she gently pushed me back and said, "I guess we'll be seeing more of you."

I was spellbound under the hypnotic effects of the shrew who was playing me like a fine-tuned piano. Strangely enough, I did not mind it one bit. What wouldn't a man do for Ms. Right Now, not Ms. Right? That's how I viewed the odds: my ultimate chance for a short-lived but long-remembered amorous adventure. Serious effort but no serious commitment, since I was firmly married to my career and divorce from purpose was a remote possibility at this point.

Nadia looked tired and washed-out after this long board meeting. She had the responsibility of directing the troops once the chairman called for battle. I could tell from the look on her face that the Madeira affair was no small task to accomplish. However,

I genuinely thought this matter blown out of proportion. Apparently, only clerical irregularities were behind the problems. Any high-powered law firm in Madrid would have fixed this in no time. Why all the fuss, and why this ad hoc inquisitive task force headed by this shady Iranian character and (little) me?

Nadia explained that the casino was clean and profitable and that there were no material reasons for the gaming commission to single it out. Her reasoning seemed in harmony with my hunch. The casino was 60% owned by Inter-Finance and 40% owned by the Al-Huzaidis, a powerful merchant family from Kuwait. The current management was entrusted to a Latino fellow by the colorful name of Manuel Eduardo Artensio. His family was involved in running casinos in Cuba before their forced exile by the cigar-smoking, US-bashing, banana-munching bearded dictator. El Jefe! According to Nadia, Manuel was every thing you would expect from a casino manager. Suave, loyal, good with high rollers, and every bit a polished gentleman. My brief was to accompany Cyrus, take notes, and wait for additional instructions from Nadia or the chairman. No further intelligence or instructions were offered for now.

On our way to Spain, Cyrus told me in no uncertain terms that his loyalty was to the chairman and not to Inter-Finance. Cyrus added that the chairman viewed me--despite my short tenure in the "shop"--as a member of his inner circle. I immediately felt guilty by association. No valid reasons supported my sudden feeling of culpability, only my instincts. The flight to Spain was a pleasant journey during which I learned more about Cyrus. He and the chairman were classmates at Oxford (which proves my point that anyone could get into the Ivy League or the Oxbridge schools, right?). They bonded on the banks of some nearby river and most probably defrauded few banks since. They became inseparable from time immemorial. Cyrus's family was involved in banking in Iran under the Shah. Their holdings in Bank Melli Iran were but a vestige of their pre-revolutionary wealth. Cyrus was a die-hard bachelor who liked to party and work with the same intensity: in short, a maniac whose favorite hobbies were polo and Eurasian girls. His knowledge of gambling was very limited. As he put it, he had watched *Casino Royale* five times and never understood the plot. I wasn't comforted by Cyrus's answer, but then I was almost sure that our direct skills were not the rationales behind us ending up with this assignment. A Persian playboy and a rookie lawyer are obviously not your best choices to resolve the mystery of an Andalusian imbroglio.

The Madeira Casino was an L-shaped ten stories building with an outside swimming pool surrounded by neatly scattered bungalows reserved for guests and VIPs. Manuel Eduardo Artensio was waiting for us at the main gate, and greeted us accompanied by two Spanish goddesses sent from the highest heavens to soothe our long journey into this rumbling Eden. Ever the dandy, Manuel was dressed in a white silk suit that gave him a Barry Manilow look, but thank goodness without the dreadful voice.

The lobby was a magnificent display of cross-cultures, a true mosaic of civilizations. There was a replica of the Dying Bull of Picasso in all its splendor in the center room, a collection of fine Persian rugs tossed by the dozens over a red crimson floor, a French Baccarat chandelier big enough to light a football stadium, exotic flower arrangements with an enchanting aroma and baskets of roses, giant, and all this Hollywood-like scene was played to the tune of the feisty music of *Carmen*--that petite brunette in short skirt who multiplied lovers and teased bullfighters!

No wonder that only Bizet, a Frenchman, would have thought of such tragic story for an opera, only to actually die during one of its rehearsals. (Check it out, it is historically true.)

Dinner was served with splendor and exquisite taste. Manuel, Cyrus, and I were joined by Manuel's girls (meaning for the dumb readers, ladies of doubtful repute but of infinite legs and charisma—yes, charisma, damn it!). When the dinner ended the troika gathered in Manuel's office, which overlooked the gaming tables. Manuel started by saying that the casino had fallen behind some new regulations that recently came into effect, and which limited betting margins to available capital. Sort of a lending-to-capital ratio, as applied in banks. He told us how he managed liquidity, how many high rollers he had invited this month, and spoke of general issues. Nothing serious, really. Then he continued by saying that the newly appointed Chairman of the Gaming Commission--Javier Del Tulipa, a fierce Catalan--suddenly threatened to close the whole operation because of some alleged irregularities. Even a temporary closure would have dire consequences for the casino. The gaming commission had requested client names, statistics, and other data not requested in the normal course of business. Rumor had it that the socialist government wanted to curb corruption and control bribery by closely monitoring political opponents, who could be siphoning money from touristic outlets such as the casino. Manuel had no problem with the disclosure request of the commission except for the clients' scores. That would blow the anonymity, the sacred trade of casino business. Furthermore, the gaming commission was insisting on a capital increase. The casino, as we understood, was doing rather well and its liquidity position was better than many in Spain. A capital increase by Inter-Finance and the Al-Huzaidis was not a very welcome matter at this critical time when the Persian Gulf War was raging. One could only imagine the Gulf newspapers' headlines scooping about a capital investment in a satanic business by the Kuwaitis under the corrupt influence of the degenerate West. Heads would roll instead of dice—literally, that is.

We had all the evening to think and contemplate. Cyrus decided to call it an early evening and I decided to wander in the gardens of the casino. Here where I stood in the middle of the night, thousands of years ago stood my ancestors, conquerors of Andalusia and princes of the desert. They left so many trails behind them, so many signs of greatness: palaces, gardens, schools, universities, and libraries.

Territories were named after them: Gibraltar or Jabal Tareq, Guadalajara or Wadi El Hijara, and countless other locations that left their imprints in this former empire that would leave an etymology specialist to gaze in awe. And here I was taking part in the rescue operation of a gambling outfit…in decadent times, dealing with unscrupulous characters, in a corruption-laden Iberian peninsula. The job I was about to begin was nothing close to a nobleman who riding his white steed and wearing the colors of his tribe to conquer the land, save the souls, and forever capture the spirit of these majestic surroundings. I might conquer one of Manuel's girls, save some money, and capture some thieves, but spirits never.

My mind could not stop wandering. Firstly, the name of Javier Del Tulipa sounded familiar. Where had I heard this name before? Maybe I was confusing him with someone else. Secondly, insisting on the identities of high rollers under the pretext of fighting corruption is not of the province of the gaming commission. The special tax division might be the more suitable agency to investigate bribery. Thirdly, a cash injection could not have been called-for at a worse time. The Al-Huzaidis were not strictly observant, but funding a gambling operation during the Iran-Iraq war was not the best PR campaign. Why hadn't our Spanish counsel been involved in this matter? The firm of Esteban, Rosa & Miguel was a powerful Madrid law firm, with connections into the highest echelons of the establishment. Seriously, a few discreet phone calls could have been sufficient to put this matter and our minds to rest.

I was nowhere close to solving this riddle when I headed back to my room. It was 1:30 a.m. and I was unable to sleep. I decided to read an old issue of *The Economist* that I picked up from the lobby. I have great respect for this publication; however, I really do not believe the Brits, whose economy is in shambles, ought to give anyone else good advice on how to run theirs. Although such colonial magazine is a rare breed, I find its pompous tone and lecture-like articles quite a bore in this CNN age. Boredom kept me from sleeping. I needed to be either tired or drunk to quickly fall asleep. I was neither. So I decided to take a shower to calm my senses and soothe my body.

It must have been a combination of my awful and loud singing that covered the sounds of an intruder into my room. But from my vantage point in the shower, I started to hear footsteps. Someone was searching the drawers, now the unpacked luggage--and finally, looking under the bed. The bathroom was foggy, I was naked, and the only weapon I could think of was the towel, which I used to better means by wrapping my waist and preparing to burst into the room to surprise my uninvited guest. The moment I turned the doorknob the noise stopped. I opened the door and was face to face with one of Manuel's girls. You know. One of the Lolitas I told you about earlier. She was not a bit surprised and instead looked at me with ease and a bit of malice. The thick fake gold cross hanging from her neck and buried into her cleavage did not make her saintly to me.

"Buenas noce, Señorita," I said in my broken Spanish. "Can I be of any help? Is it the grail you are after or some other holier item?"

Her reply showed an above average knowledge of medieval history. "The grail it ain't," she retorted, "but I wouldn't mind a Percival for tonight."

Sylvana Massotto was instructed by Manuel to search my room, looking for his pink slip. The poor Cubano thought that he was being fired by Inter-Finance and that Cyrus and I were the undertakers. He did not realize that such matters were nowadays expedited by a cold facsimile message wishing him better luck in greener pastures.

I reassured Sylvana that such matter was not in the offing, and that her Manuel was not about to be castrated professionally. Sylvana smiled and said that uno, he was not "her" Manuel, and that duo, castration was not her favorite subject at 2:00 a.m. with me next to her, and tres, that I should stop moving back toward the wall and instead come closer and kiss her. No wonder that Spanish men have to fight bulls for a hobby. With the type of women they have at home, I think bullfighting is just about the right training.

Have you ever been to heaven? What a silly question, you must be saying to yourself, of course not. Wrong! Heaven is not where the clouds are white, the sky is blue, and the angels sing. Heaven is where the sheets are white, your face is blue, and the only things that sing are bed screws which would surely need greasing or replacing after tonight. Sylvana was not the talkative type. Sylvana was not the moaning type. Sylvana was simply the right type. Blazingly hot, rebellious, and always on the move. For a moment I had reclaimed a great piece of [A]....ndalusia. One has to start somewhere, and Sylvana was my favorite passageway into this sensual conquest. Granted, the jewelry was fake, but the orgasms were real, or so they sounded....

In the morning, Cyrus was waiting for me in the restaurant, by the pool. Breakfast was only served starting at 10:00 a.m. Prior to such time, all casino guests (and all of Spain for that matter) were asleep. Cyrus had spoken to the chairman the night before. I wondered when, since the last time I saw him he was in his Jacuzzi with more Asian girls than a Louis Vuitton shop. The chairman arranged for us to meet in the afternoon with a certain Jack Brooks, an American journalist who had been living in Spain since the bells last tolled. In the meantime I was expected to go over certain documents with Manuel in order to unearth any false reporting or irregularities in the casino's books.

We ate, and headed to Manuel's private office. While dreading to see red lights, cheap (or Turkish, for the experts) leather furniture, black carpeting and white Angora cats, we saw a different picture altogether. After all this, the Cubano was able to smuggle some of his family belongings on the banana boat over to Florida. The rugs were made of an amazing combination of colored Peruvian quilts. The Spanish old-style chairs and the ebony wood desk were worthy of El Caudillo's office (don't tell the Passionara I said that) and the picture of the family's tobacco farm "La Sultana" added a touch of old roots and authenticity that Manuel's diamond ring clearly lacked.

Manuel was anxious. He had that look of King Louis XVI at the sight of the giant head cutter that was on display at the Place de la Bastille. Indeed, it was displayed long enough to cause more royal damage during 1789 than had the London tabloids in the 1980s, if that was humanly possible. Manuel reiterated that all the casino's accounts were audited semi-annually, carefully reviewed at each interval by management, and diligently compiled by counsel prior to their filing with the gaming commission. To the best of our advisers' knowledge, the casino had no inaccurate, false or misleading statement in its filings. You have suspected I guess (and do not betray the benefit of intelligence I am bestowing upon you) that all such documents were written in Spanish (including the financial statements). Indeed, I hadn't the faintest clue whether Manuel was showing me his dentist's bill or the maintenance report on the slot machines. In order to limit the confusion--and the time required for me to learn the language of the Conquistadors--we decided to request from the law firm of Esteban, Rosa & Miguel a cover-your-ass-with-a-double-blanket legal opinion (yes, in English, you fools!) regarding all filings with the gaming commission.

A teleconference was arranged with Mr. Rosa and the conversation was (I suppose) carried out in English--or come to think of it, in "Spanglish." Mr. Rosa was a "can do" type of attorney who belonged to the old Chico's network that stretched from the king's palace to ETA's upper circles (the Basque separatist movement for the non-politically-attuned readers). He seemed genuinely concerned about the motives of this official inquiry. He was baffled because his buddy, the Minister of Tourism and the direct boss of the Chairman of the Gaming Commission, had no reasons to squeeze this hotel in particular. The minister was a prime beneficiary of the casino's largesse--namely, Lola the Stripper, whose melons he squeezed every other Thursday in one of the casino's bungalows. We had all the reels to prove it. The heat, according to Mr. Rosa, should be coming from the special taxation division (STD) that was in charge of all foreign-owned entities operating in Spain. It seemed, according to Mr. Rosa, that the casino's dealings were perfectly legit. But, it felt as if a secret war was being waged, with the casino as its main battleground.

After the legal jargon was over, we started questioning Manuel a propos the clientele of the casino. As if to give the discussion more importance, and to add a touch of secrecy, Manuel lowered the lights, closed the doo,r and came closer to me. Remember these are the very moves that I would indulge in if I had Christine Keeler (not Julia Roberts, you cheap movie-goers) in my office. Manuel must have felt more comfortable in the dim lights--maybe because his low IQ would not shine so brightly in darker surroundings? Manuel recalled a certain conversation he had few months back with a shady business-man named Daniel Fardi. He was a rich but mysterious fellow living in Spain. Fardi wanted to rent bungalows at the casino for some visiting rollers. He insisted on their getting a special treatment at the tables. At first Manuel did not understand his request and thought that Fardi wanted his clients to "win" so he could hook them and then stage a high-stakes game to clean them out, with the casino aiding in the plot. But Fardi had the opposite in mind. He wanted them to lose, and even asked for nothing in return. That again did not seem right to Manuel, who informed Fardi that the casino did not and would not accommodate any "fixing" of games. The reason why Manuel mentioned this story was because Daniel's nose was spotted on several occasions since they last spoke, pointing in the face of a high official of the STD. Was Daniel getting even because Manuel frustrated his plans? But if so, why would he be talking to this governmental agency? Why would this Fardi character (carrying an Israeli passport, mind you) want his friends to lose, and why would the STD care? I kept Manuel talking for a while, hoping to find a clue that would glue together this awfully loose plot. It finally came from an unsuspected piece of info. A request in Daniel's reservation form addressed to the casino and that was in Manuel's files. Daniel had sent a reservation request (in Spanish, yes) including dates of arrivals, room types, and special meals. I did not immediately notice that "mini bar" meant the same in all hotels. On Daniel's original request it was expressly stated that the rooms should have no mini bars. I didn't think much of it at first until Manuel read to me more strange demands formulated by Daniel and concerning the stay of his friends at the casino.

What Manuel did not realize was that Daniel's friends were most probably Iranian officials. How would these characters mingle together? Talk about Poisonous Jaffa Oranges and Arsenic-peppered Caviar, all in one platter. At first glance this might have been confusing (but it is meant to be, you slow- thinking brats!). When Daniel insisted that his guests be kept in the semi-reclusive suites located in the back of the hotel, no TV, or Western music was to be played, no booze and no girls to be allowed nearby, it started making much more sense, to me. Only two people in the world would prefer to live in such self-imposed quarantine when offered the magnificent surroundings of the Madeira Casino: the Dalai Lama and Iranian mullahs.

The Dalai Lama, to my knowledge has not been labeled (so far) as a compulsive gambler. The only game he insists on playing is "Chinese Roulette" year after year!

But the alternative of Iranians was as unfounded as my first guess. I recalled no defections from the "Rug Curtain" since the Iranian revolution. No relaxation of morals and no paid vacation in sunny Costa del Sol for their tieless, bearded diplomats. What were the Bazaris doing with a son of Moses' tribes in this Iberian Sodom and Gomorrah? Daniel's name added to my curiosity. He was not a Butowsky (from Poland) or an Eisenberg (from Austria); instead he was a Fardi. I figured that the uninitiated Manuel (and especially my beloved readers) would not pick up such a clue. A Fardi, my fellow (but still unequal) readers, is the name of a prominent Jewish banking family from Damascus. They were forced to travel from Southern Spain (how bizarre) as most Sephardic Jews did, to Fez, then to Damascus. How would I know that? I recalled one of my uncles telling me about their neighbors: the Fardis. The family finally settled in Beirut just before the declaration of the State of Israel in 1948. Were the Iranians some distant cousins of Daniel's tribe? Khomeini held no sons of Zion close to his heart and vice versa. I was dead set on pursuing Daniel's trail and much closer.

Once in Spain, do like the Spaniards do. But they don't do, that is. They practice the *siesta*. It is not a daily routine, but a life philosophy. The notion of *siesta* shredded to pieces all of my Lutheran values that proselytized the beginning of each dawn with honest, hard work that lasted till dusk. Work was a way of expressing one's respect for, and faith in, the Almighty. And the Almighty would bestow rewards. But life turned unfair for many hardworking people. The Swiss have worked endlessly to bring us precision watches only to be remembered for the cuckoo clock. They've built a formidable defense industry only to be credited for a red multi-purpose yet totally useless army knife. Whereas the Spaniards did nothing literally and worshiped dead time through the *siesta* and yet got immortalized by Goya, Gaudi, Dali, Picasso, and many others? Name one famous Swiss! Go figure that one out, Mr. Luther.

At such hour, a Bacardi/Diet Coke (for those to whom Cuba Libre would have sounded like a battleship from Havana) coupled with a view of the mountain under a bright southern sun predisposed me for an indulgence in Spain's national sport: a good old nap.

Jack Brooks looked like Jimmy Stewart, but in relaxed clothes and without the '50s hat. Jack was a very good acquaintance of our chairman, amongst other people. His stated profession as a freelance journalist in Costa Del Sol was sufficient to provoke suspicions about his real occupation. He received us in his office chomping a cigar and sipping a tall glass of lemonade. Jack greeted us warmly and explained that Rutger Zarmat had spoken to him only in general terms about our issue. He asked us to candidly explain the "perceived" problem at the casino. So we did. He listened carefully to our version of events, pausing at intervals to give certain sequences of the story more attention. He knew that the casino was running smoothly and that Manuel, albeit a gigolo, was a decent individual. He heard no complaints about the management or about any shady activities at the tables. Jack, as we learned, was very close to the STD; hence, Rutger's call for help. The chairman wanted to circle the wagon: Rosa would cover the Ministry of Tourism and Jack the STD. Cyrus asked Jack about the probable cause behind the official inquiry, maybe thinking that the Yankee would spill the beans for free. He simply wasn't disposed to do so, and I fully understood his position. That kind of intelligence cannot be bought like pistachios in a Tehran bazaar, by the kilo, but instead like pearls, one piece at a time.

I interjected and inquired whether Jack could arrange for us to meet with Daniel Fardi. "Sure," he replied. I was startled by his spontaneous answer, but glad that I had punched a hole in this riddle. Jack did not hesitate in responding, nor did he ask about my motives for seeking to meet a person whose name was not mentioned in our 1.5-hour-long conversation. It was all I needed to know. The circle of friends was slowly closing in. We left his office feeling tired but satisfied, me especially.

At 7:00 p.m. I was dozing off in my room when the phone rang. Jack's voice on the other end was suave, as if he were picking up a hottie at the champagne bar at the Royalton Hotel in New York. You know that kind of husky voice that wants to inspire confidence, maintain self-respect, and use intimidation before screwing you. Jack had fixed a dinner party at his house at 10:00 p.m. Fardi would be there. *That was quick*, I thought. He would send his driver to pick us up at around 9:30 p.m. from the hotel. There was not one minute to waste. I called Cyrus and we both called the chairman. Rutger was cold, but sounded relieved that Jack agreed to help. He figured that if Jack was pitching in some help, then someone from the other side of the tracks--be it Fardi or the STD--was willing to deal. Some kind of quid pro quo was involved, he insisted. Someone needed a favor; otherwise Jack would not have picked up this assignment. You have to know that Jack was the quintessential middleman. I genuinely believe that the day he was born, he must have negotiated his smooth entry into the world with the doctors. "You'll charge half price, I'll stop kicking, and we'll forget all about C-section." My far-fetched theory about the Iranians sounded logical to Rutger. I myself could not comprehend how by connecting Israelis to Iranians to gambling, things would look lucid. Rutger asked that Jack be the one making the intro and for me (not Cyrus) to do the talking. The reason was less his belief in my negotiating skills and more in letting me cut a "first draft" before the final deal. Boy, did I feel better with that last piece of explanatory comment--an uncalled-for assertion of my rookie status...a certificate of my single-digit IQ painted in neon lights and hanging from Times Square on New Year's Eve.

We arrived at Jack's home, which was a classic hacienda turned into a *Miami Vice* bad character's mansion: mustachioed guards at the door who smelled fresh fajitas, the customary Doberman greetings with saliva to boot, the luxury cars with the wrong colors (the white Ferrari, the red Porsche and the three- mile-long yellow submarine...or was it a limo?). Jack greeted us standing tall at the gate. You could tell from the Gloria Estefan/Mambo Kings music that the evening was going to be hot, as all Latino parties are supposed to be. (When I said hot, your twisted minds went on wsndering between the thighs of Linda Evangelista and bikinis of pre-Castro dancers at the Copa Cabana). I only mentioned hot because of the spicy food (including baby food)! Have you ever heard of frosted jalapeños or tortillas crispies? If not, then both your palate and your neighborhood are safe for now. The huge living room was abuzz with fancy dresses and expert un-dressers. You know the type. Give me any complex bra mechanism and I'll free it in under three seconds. The "Houdinis of Underwear."

After some casual chat, Jack whisked us into a private study. Daniel Fardi was seated in a long chair halfway through into his drink and his desert female Oryx. The Israeli army is filled with that type of mammal, I was told--a mixture of a dancing Salome and a whistling Lauren Bacall. Greetings were exchanged and Jack did not lose time beating around the bush. He invited us to speak freely. Daniel dismissed his girl and turned to us with a large appealing smile. "Gentlemen, I believe you wanted to talk to me about the casino."

I took the (big) initiative with my (little) authority to transact this business. "We believe that we have common interests," I went on, explaining: "The casino, since we both need its services, it seems." I began my spiel by stressing the business standards of Inter-Finance and the ethics it followed in doing business worldwide. I then quickly digressed to the casino and explained that we had full confidence in Manuel. That no funny business was going on and that our lawyer, Mr. Rosa, would soon provide us with a legal opinion that supports our standings vis-à-vis the STD. My killjoy discourse distracted Daniel, who showed signs of impatience. So I went for the kill. "You have sought some services from the casino; they were obviously denied; and soon thereafter the STD came down heavily on us. So we have reason to believe that your intervention in this matter was more than a coincidence. Without denying or recognizing any role in this mess, we would like to better understand what exactly you want?"

"A reconsideration, eh?" inquired Daniel with a slimy smile.

"Frankly, I am not paid to negotiate but to close," I retorted.

I had no intention of letting Fardi win this argument or savor his victory for having brought us to the negotiation table.

Daniel adjusted himself in the seat, as if to enjoy the show, and said, "A true scion of the Kadi clan." For a moment I thought that I was going to faint. The silence that gripped the room could be heard miles away. He had just mentioned my grandfather's name. (This doesn't help you, does it? You are smart readers, but not yet psychics). Daniel hurried his explanation to the benefit of everyone. It so happened that my grandfather, who was a judge, had helped Daniel's family obtain a money-changing license in Beirut prior to 1948, out of which they went on to build a banking business. And then again, in 1967 my grandfather assisted Daniel's family to sell their business, and most importantly to get a renewal of their passports for them to exit the country and immigrate to Brazil. For a split second I saw Nadia Gotryne's face. She must have dug into the family's records and suggested to Rutger Zarmat that he use me on this transaction. From that moment onward, Daniel was very friendly. He asked if we could talk in private and Cyrus obliged. Only then did Daniel spill the beans.

The Iranians were expecting a massive attack from the Iraqi forces on Khoramshahr, a port city located approximately 10 kilometers (6.2 mi) north of Abadan. The city extends to the right bank of the Arvandrud Waterway near its confluence with the Haffar arm of the Karun river. Their victory in this anticipated battle against the forces of Saddam Hussein, the Iraqi tyrant, or even their mere survival would be a turning point in the Iraq-Iran war. Saddam's forces were pounding them with all their might. Khoramshahr was impregnable by ground troops due to the nature of the terrain and the fortifications in place. However, the

Iraqis had acquired a sophisticated Chinese-made tank called "Trojan." The Trojans had the double function of piercing into fortified areas and unloading fresh troops. The tanks carried devastating anti-carriers and anti-personnel rockets. They additionally had the capacity of carrying up to twelve fighting men, which saved the Iraqis time to hurry troops behind their tanks, eliminating the need for heavier armored vehicles. Anti-Trojan rockets had been effectively tested by the Israelis Defense Forces (IDF) for quite some time now with a 99.99% success rate. The "Kedesh" hand-held missile was light to carry, easy to operate, and abundantly available at IDF's warehouses in Jaffa. From Jaffa harbor they could be shipped to Khoramshahr on Dvora boats (the Hebrew version of the Nazi U-boats) to avoid Iraq's radar detection devices.

I was still perplexed. How would the Israelis deliver state-of-the art weaponry to their sworn enemies in Tehran? Daniel continued his story. The Kedeshs were retailing at $3750 apiece, and the bearded mullahs had placed an order for 100,000 pieces totaling $375 million (for those who failed their math tests amongst you and have taken up a career in government, running budget deficits). Furthermore, the Iranians were willing to pay in cash in two installments: one at shipment and one at delivery. I figured out (all by myself) that the exchange would not be in the form of a bank check or a wire transfer. For more reasons why, ask the Pahlavis, Marcoses, and the Bhuttos about Swiss banking secrecy when you are an out-of-favor dictator.

The plot was painfully simple. The Iranians would play at the casino and quietly lose a modest sum of $375 million. Daniel's cousins would, on the other hand, win almost the exact sum of the money lost. The casino would pocket a 5% commission and transfer the funds from the fake losers, to the equally fake win-ners. Daniel went on explaining to me why Cyrus was not to be privy to this matter since he had no love lost for the chaps running the show in Persia. Daniel knew that he could trust me due to family ties and the good deeds of the past. However, I in turn knew why Rutger Zarmat had insisted on Cyrus being around. He could be a potential whistle-blower should things go wrong. Cyrus was wired to all CIA operatives south of Rome. He could blow this deal to pieces had Zarmat told him to do so, thus severely damaging the chances of a serious arms deal by the Khomeni regime. The Israelis, on the other hand, loathed Saddam and wanted to maintain the equilibrium of terror between both camps. Uncle Sam did not disagree too much with this kill, and let them be killed policy. Scorpions in a bottle, so to speak. Now that everyone had a finger in the pie no one planned on eating it, yet. They needed the kitchen--the casino, that is. Once we were on board, it was time to play ball.

Talking about playing ball, a loud scream took our minds and hearts away from our discreet business. We joined the rest of the party and the voices guided us into a corridor that led to a study. A huge TV screen was hanging from the wall with Pavarotti sing-ing "Passione" with no sound, only subtitles. There, sitting in the middle of the room was a large man whose testicles were trapped in an old-fashioned nutcracker. Two beautiful ladies from each side were operating the torture engine, pushing it a little harder when requested by the crowd, and the poor man in turn would oblige by singing with a pain-induced baritone voice. To ease the pain, bags of ice cubes were set under the seat and another lady, feather in hand, intermittently stroked the imprisoned genitalia to extract a mixture of pain and pleasure. The singing quality was surprisingly close to the original work. A near-perfect Karaoke party. So don't complain next time you pay a $100 ticket to watch some fat man sing opera. He earned every cent of it so you can keep every inch of yours.

Back at the hotel, Cyrus went to his emerging Asian girls and I longed for the bar, only to find it half empty with a replica of Celia Cruz singing on stage surrounded by a group of Cubans. They were presided over by none other than dear old Manuel. He waved from afar and invited me to join the boys for a last drink. I eagerly accepted after noticing that all were not just boys. I sat facing a girl who was introduced to me by Manuel as "Lucinda," the premier croupier of the casino. Lucinda was Manuel's second cousin from Havana, where her family managed a lesser gaming outlet. She grew up in Miami playing cards since she was four, and had been probably qualified as a "man eater" from the day she was born. Lucinda will make you lose your mind at first sight. And it does not take a deck of cards to do so. Any deck would do. Even copper decks in old Amsterdam. Lucinda, smelling my desire from afar, ventured closer to me. I was chatting with Manuel while she stared at me, with apparent malice. My heart was beating faster than Tito Puente's drummer. Lucinda moved her chair toward me whilst oscillating like a cobra in a Marrakech Souk, at the sound of her flutist charmer. The cobra's body first elongates in a swirling fashion, then the back rounds up, giving it all the forward motion needed; the neck stretches out, and finally the tongue makes a stinging sortie. So did Lucinda sting me, and like the cobra she retracted and, excusing herself to the restroom, left me dumbfounded and speechless.

I took this quiet moment to bring Manuel up to speed on the arrangement that we had sealed with Daniel. Given that the sum in question was no small change, many actors would have to take part in the scheme. The games would be staged in three nights, at three different tables, simulating a perfect losing/winning streak. The Iranians would lose big while the Israelis would win it all. Roulette and blackjack were the chosen games.

This scheme was to remain ultra-secret from all, including, but most importantly the Kuwaiti co-owners. It was agreed to entrust Lucinda with supervising the games. Manuel would fix the tables. Jack would be in charge of transferring the chips from the rollers to the casino cashier, making a short stop at the kitchen to deduct our fees, and the gains would end up in IDF's vaults. Daniel would accompany the players. Cyrus would watch their tongues to interpret any last-minute reversals. Yoram Mirador (the Mossad's most trusted killer after Raffi Eitan) would get the cash safely out of the country. I was there to make sure that Inter-Finance took its 5% tip in colored chips. Jack's fees--in addition to a small token for a high official at the STD--would come out of our share.

Lucinda re-emerged from the restroom more relaxed then when she went in. Naturally, she forgot to wipe out the cocaine dust from her nose and looked as if she had stuck her face in a Bulgari powder box (or was it Vulgari?). Cocaine is called angel dust. Well, it wakes the devil in me. That is on the morality level. On the sexual front it puts me off. Lucinda would not believe it. She could not understand why I was suddenly aloof and cold. I explained the reason and she started laughing. I stood my ground and excused myself, leaving behind a sensual woman with a frozen look, but not from the shock of rejection, I presumed. I was really pissed at her. She was young, good-looking, and smart. I was well-disposed to answer her mating call with a roar that would put Tarzan to shame. Natural sex was a drug by itself, so why spoil it with additives that look like a thinly crushed chalk ration in a ziplock bag! I am an ecologist at heart, a flesh-eaterian par excellence. I firmly believe that dim halogen lights, silk white linens, music, Veuve Clicquot champagne, scented creams during and fresh towels after, are the secret for an unforgettable evening with Lucinda (or whomever).

Especially that night, I could not sleep. The events of the day were running in my head and the adrenaline infusion in my body was having an extra filling. A war was being waged miles away from this pleasant resort. People were going at each other's throats, families were being dislocated and villages wiped out, towns besieged, fortunes lost and made, legions annihilated, and societies scarred forever. I was in a no small part a facilitator and a cheat by advancing dubious rationales. "All wars are dirty," I said to myself. "The Iran-Iraq conflict will keep the rest of the Gulf in peace," I further argued. We are restoring the balance of power between the protagonists. We're making a handsome profit! See, that was the kind of deduction that gave me an instant doze of satisfaction and put me to sleep in an exhilarated mood. In the middle of the night I woke up again. "We're making a profit?! Who's 'we'? Idiot!" I slept on a millionaire's dream just to wake up to a beggar's reality. I was not making a dime on this deal. Nobody even hinted at my take, my portion, my pound of flesh. With that in mind, I could not close my eyes.

I snapped into action and called Lucinda's room. I was intent on making peace with my moral soul. Was I a preacher? "Pat Robertson would do the same," I said, "and I am no better than Pat." If Lucinda would consent me doing to her what she was doing to her brains, then that was perfectly all right with me. Lucinda, as a good Catholic, feeling morally vindicated and absolved by my approbation came in an instant (to my room, that is, you morons!!) Lucinda was wearing a short summer dress. They call them frontier dresses because they start at the edge of the bosom and end at the limit of the behind. She smelled like sandalwood and felt like a warm bath after a hard day's work. She was sober, apparently cleaned up, and refreshingly happy. The rest of that evening is the province of my memory, and you will permit me not to share the details of my intimate encounters in public. Especially on this occasion.

The next three days went on as planned. The security was beefed up from all sides. Daniel and I were watching over the unfolding of events. A trust level was finally established among all protagonists. I must add that besides fear, greed played a good part in securing the success of this bargain. The ongoing trade was too valuable to jeopardize because of ideology, faith, or simple bravado. In the casino kitchen, Jack, Daniel, Cyrus, and I counted the chips, segregated the middlemen's fees, and took the rest. The chairman had insisted on cash payment in the form of chips only to be exchanged later in hard cash over a number of weeks. We diligently complied with his request.

Our last day in Spain would haunt me for the rest of my life. We had finished our business, checked out of the hotel, and checked into the VIP lounge at the private airport when Manuel, clearly showing signs of distress, barged in. We probed him about whether the deal was in trouble. Manuel dismissed our queries with a simple nod, but still could not speak. Then, he sat down and burst into tears. Lucinda had been found dead in one of the casino's bungalows. No signs of sexual abuse or bodily injury were detected. Her nose was bleeding from the excessive sniffing of cocaine, apparently. A large quantity of the drug was found in her room. But Lucinda did not have the kind of money to buy a large slag, Manuel said. Someone must have given her the dust! A horribly gripping pain immediately spread throughout my body. I could not breathe, could not move; I was numb as if put on ice. My mind was working at Mach II. Someone had set to erase all tracks, and Lucinda was the weakest link in the chain. Hence, she was disposable. By the same token, her death would send a sufficiently strong warning for anyone who dared recount the details of our venture, even in their sleep.

Lucinda did not die from an overdose; she was a casual user, not an addict. We had spoken about that the night before, and she had no reason to lie to me before trusting me with her inner self. You see, men lie before making love, but women don't. Men fabricate stories about their jobs, their sexual prowess, and how nice they will be after the act. Women have a nasty habit of listening before and comparing notes after.

The Iranians could not have done it, because it was not their style. They find it immoral (I do too) to kill a woman. What could she possibly do to harm them? It couldn't have been Daniel, either, since he could exert pressure on the casino without going to such extremes. The only unsavory character in this play was Yoram Mirador, the Mossad's henchman and expert user of knives. Folks like him were trained to kill and leave no traces behind. He must have done his "dirty" work on the way out after having secured the shipment of funds. Mossad was highly skilled in making a premeditated murder look like an unfortunate accident--or better, a self-inflicted wound, as in Lucinda's case.

Returning home, I could not forget Lucinda's angelic face, her trusting smile. I was happy that I did not detail the intimate moments of our encounter. They belonged to another world now. But I was intent on getting even with Yoram and I prayed that God would give me that opportunity. Back on the 14th floor, Mrs. Gotryne showered me with praises, words of comfort, and congrats from the chairman. Having had my share of moral credit, I was expecting some sort of payment in kind--and not in kindness! But I quickly learned that rich people rarely pay; they'd rather make a pledge!

OF ICE AND MEN

The doorbell awakened me. I checked the time; it was 5:00 p.m. I must have dozed off after lunch. The culprit was the empty vodka bottle next to my bed. For a second, my mind visualized Soviet troops fighting the Cold War armed with vodka only. Suddenly, all was clear. What was the secret for Russia, a nation on the brink of bankruptcy, with an army suffering from chronic rust in its tanks and top brass? In a flashpoint that secret was revealed to me. The Russians were neither overprepared nor overconfident; they simply were drunk!! What else could explain their brinkmanship during the Cuban missile crisis? Or the Afghan invasion? Vodka.

Back to my immediate theatre of operations, I ran to the door and opened it only wearing my boxer shorts to see an angel appear before me. Here she was, Soraya, the early-morning breeze, standing with a majestic look and a bright smile that lit her tanned face. "May I come in?" she whispered. I obliged without further ado and rushed to my room to wear something decent. I returned in T-shirt and shorts. Soraya handed me a thick red file titled: "Crown Jewels." At first I thought that it was some museum exhibit to which I was invited. Wrong! That was a package sent by the chairman through Mrs. Gotryne for a quick review and reporting. Soraya was eager to leave and I was equally inclined to reverse this course of action. So I politely--for a change--invited her to have something to drink before she headed back home (I presumed?).

"I seldom drink," she said. I assured her of my bewilderment at her camel-like habits. She burst into laughter and agreed to have tea. Here we go again with my prejudices about beverages: Tea. Who drinks it? No, really. I can only imagine myself drinking tea when: (a) seriously ill with a sour throat to save on cold medicine, or (b) invited by the old bugger at Buckingham Palace 'cause 'tis good manners, or (c) at gunpoint in Afghanistan with a crowd of Talibanis hurling AK47s. Why on earth would anyone with sound mind and sane body want to drink tea? Coffee gives you a buzz. It makes you look like the Marlboro man in a Grand Canyon scene. On the other hand, men who drank tea had taken piano lessons (if not ballet, too) when they were kids, owned a pet cat called "Maribel," and played bingo with their grandparents, at the parish hall, every Sunday afternoon.

One tea to go for Soraya! I fixed the tea in seconds, not to miss Soraya's company while boiling water and pouring herbs into mugs. When I returned, gentle Soraya was exploring my library, as often people do when they first visit--as if one could guess the level of your intellect just from glancing at your books. Let me quash this fallacy. In most instances, books in libraries are in sync with the furniture, so one buys them for the looks, not the content. Now you tell me that everyone that bought the Encyclopedia Brittanica has read it! Yeah, sure. Let's assume for a moment that one has a few hundred books. That, if anything, is not a sign of intelligence. You might have read these books and had no clue of their meaning. Or you might not even have read them at all. What's the point, then, in examining one's library? Let me enlighten your cavern-like minds. First, it is a ploy to kill time intelligently when an idiot is fixing you tea. Second, you can score points by saying you have read some of this stuff so you can look bright and learned. Third and the most relevant argument to me, it is useful for picking conversation in tough spots!

"Your books are well-varied in authors and subjects," said Soraya. Yes! She was picking up conversation.

"I never have the time to read them, so I just collect them for my retirement," I replied.

"On that intelligent-sounding note, let us have some tea and biscuits," she said with sarcasm dripping from her beautiful lips. I was still in my shorts when she decided to play ladylike and pour me a cup of tea. I was staring at her so bluntly that she shivered, lost control, and sprayed my right thigh with the liquid I had boiled just seconds ago. I opened my mouth to let out a huge scream that would put the National Alarm Siren into obsolescence only to see Soraya's lips covering my mouth with a sorry-I-made-a-hole-in-your-thigh kiss. Miracle of miracles! All the pain disappeared from my leg just to find refuge in my stomach--a burning bowl of fire ravaging my intestines and other pipes of my anatomy. Her tongue was fresh like cold water, which kept our kiss ongoing for a long period without dullness. Do you know what it means to kiss for that long and not get bored? It only means trouble. The serious kind too, the kind that gets you thinking not about the present moment but about the morning after. Some girls you fool around with, some they fool around with you. Soraya was neither. Her kind was capable of making a fool out of me. Me! Who thinks the world is his oyster, and the universe owes him apologies? This girl was my Achilles' heel. Feel free to include the rest of my body.

Our passionate kiss was no coincidence. It led to a long moment of contemplation, which ended in a gentle hug. That was a prelude to a prolonged séance of cuddling that resulted in a heated, passionate, censored for your viewing love experience. It was a blessed moment. I wanted to be anointed with Soraya's skin, embalmed with her hair, buried in her body and resurrected three hours later in my own bed with her next to me. One day, some disciples of mine, twelv3 in all, will write this story and will teach it to lovers and newlyweds around the world. Women will weep, grown men will cry, and esquires will roam the land looking for shreds of my bed linen, believing it will bring them eternal bliss.

When I woke up, Soraya was taking a shower, the music was on, and I was simply overtaken by all that had happened. Soraya appeared in my red bathrobe and sat next to me while caressing my face. I was like a child on Christmas Eve. Happy to attend, anticipating the gifts, but speechless at the sight of Santa. I did not know whether a "Thank You" would sound cheap or whether "Did you enjoy it?" would be cocky or if I should simply shut up. Soraya anticipated my thoughts and put her finger on my lips as if to prevent me from spoiling the moment for both of us. I kissed her forehead, hugged her for what seemed an eternity, and went back to sleep. When I returned back to reality she was still here, in my rocking chair, reading some magazine. I asked about the time and when I realized that it was past 9:00 p.m. I suggested dinner. We got dressed, and headed to a place with terrible food but a nice view. After dinner, we parted ways. I dropped Soraya by my apartment to get her car and followed her until she arrived safely home, kissed her goodbye, and raced back to my den.

The next morning, the 14th floor was abuzz with action. The chairman was around and all his minions were in full gear like a beehive in blossom. I was summoned into Nadia's office where a slide show was being projected. There was the treasurer of Inter-Finance, the chief legal counsel, the security expert, and Nadia. I closed the door behind me and took a seat by the screen. The show was about Inter-Finance's holdings in West Africa that included timber, copper, diamonds, and flower farms. I listened carefully to the presentation while recording the most interesting details. I had no idea how diamond rocks were extracted, polished, sold, and used. The diamond concession of Inter-Finance in Sierra Leone, NeraGem, was ninety-nine years old with sixty more to go. The concession agreement was iron clad, just like De Beers in South Africa. We operated the mine, exploited its resources, employed the local labor, ran our private army and our own court system, and operated all land and air services leading to and from the mines. The whole works. A legalized colony. We had in place a revenue-sharing arrangement netting the locals 25% of total sales. They were smart. They did not fall for our initial offer of 40% of net income, having themselves no means of controlling the expenses we would deduct before reaching the bottom line.

All our diamonds were disposed of wholesale. They were first flown to the Swiss Free Zone area and then offered to dealers from all over the world. Each of our lots was marked and sold with a certificate of origin that stated the characteristics of the lot. The certification process was very tight and suffered no exceptions. Getting diamonds into the Swiss Free Zone was conditional on having the proper certificates of origin in order to trace back all diamonds to the original mine they were extracted from. This allowed dealers to trade them on the international markets. Wholesale diamonds without a certificate of origin are called "hot" or "blood" diamonds and have no fixed value except that they traded at a deep discount to legitimate rocks. Through this certification process, local governments controlled quantities and prices that derived from each year's total productions. The control of the rough diamonds was essentially done at the mine's level. Any diamonds destined for sale by NeraGem were tagged by the concession's certification board, which was comprised of two inspectors appointed by the local treasury. They affixed the government's seal on each lot. The lots were counted, described, weighed, and transported by air under heavy security. Prior to being airborne, local customs reinspected all certificates.

Once in Switzerland, the diamonds were warehoused in the Free Zone area reserved for NeraGem. They were rechecked and re-counted by NeraGem and the government's representatives onsite. Dealers were then informed of the arrivals and invited to attend the auction. This system had been running without a glitch for decades. NeraGem had invested heavily in the mines, which employed 10% of the adult population, created trade opportunities for the country, reinvested capital in housing, roads, and dams, improved health-care conditions, and even employed a full-time environmentalist to prevent any ecological damage. For the government, this was as sure a revenue scheme as an Arabian oil concession. NeraGem's 25% of total sales were financing more than 50% of the public budget and a bit less of the unofficial one. No party to this bargain had any incentive to cheat. The more sales NeraGem generated, the more the government benefited. Inter-Finance had no reasons to tamper with this diamond-laden West African rhino (forget the golden goose).

For twenty-nine years and throughout turmoil, rebellions, coups d'état, famines, cholera, and other deadly epidemics, this system had never faltered. Not until today, that is.

The chairman entered the room and the lights went on, as of to announce his luminary presence. Next to him was an African general (I must have guessed by the color of his uniform) who was more decorated than Rockefeller Center's Christmas tree. General Abdo DiBondieu was introduced by the chairman as the strong man of Sierra Leone and a great friend of both the chairman, naturally, and of NeraGem. The general was large, with a big jaw and small bright eyes that exuded cruelty and resolve. He was seated next to Rutger and was given the floor to describe the dire straits that we were facing. In a nutshell, he started by saying, (Hold on for one second, for God's sake! Why do people assume that they can squeeze a story in a nutshell! What about the nut? Was it excused before we put the story in or consulted whether it would like to share its tiny space with some narration? No wonder why when one goes berserk he is called a nut. Now, back to the story!)

The general, as I was saying, was summarizing the situation. A few months earlier, a well-known diamonds dealer in Amsterdam named Leon Tischer, and another in London called Barry Ellis, claimed to have purchased large quantities of NeraGem's rocks. Diamond cutters in Bombay also confirmed completing some work on rocks of the same origin in recent times. So what! Everybody buys our stuff, don't they? No. According to the general and to NeraGem's records no quantities (whether large or modest) were ever sold to these dealers. NeraGem never dealt with anyone except authorized dealers whose books were regularly audited. The general further affirmed that the shady dealers apparently had authentic certificates emanating from NeraGem. The irony was that NeraGem could not challenge these dealers publicly for fear of creating panic in the market about hot diamonds. NeraGem's market value would evaporate overnight. The good news was that Leon Tischer was willing to sell us back the gems and the certificates at cost, plus a small premium of 11%. We still had to convince Barry Ellis to do the same, get the certificates back, and investigate the origin of the rocks--all in a week's time, and all in total secrecy. For the bad news part, I was put in charge of this mission. Frankly, *Mission Impossible* was a pilot show next to this task.

Nadia informed me that all the necessary data were in the "Crown Jewels" file unless I had misplaced it, in which case she could re-send Soraya to deliver it, personally. The iron lady knew about our affair and made sure that I was on high alert. Women are always good at keeping records in case they need to pull a string (not a bikini, you morons!) or two. A woman would remember what was on the menu at your first dinner, the birthdays of your best friends, and the hotel room number of your latest vacation. A man on the other hand, could only remember the day his favorite team lost the World Cup, the day he had his first threesome, and the day he saw Bo Derek in *10*. Different genders, different priorities.

The "Crown Jewels" file was very thorough, with addresses, pictures, graphs, press articles, analyses, and margin annotations. I could tell that a lawyer prepared it with a glossary, a table of contents, a disclaimer, and even an indemnification section. Damn lawyers! They are governed by certain reflexes taught in law schools and acquired during assiduous training at law firms. They naturally translate their thoughts into sentences and paragraphs suitable to any kind of occasion from finding a loophole in the Ten Commandments to arguing the rules of evidence in *Ten Little Indians*. While reading this great essay on my way to London I learned that a meeting had been arranged with Mr. Barry Ellis, at his office located at 10 Bond Street. I was authorized to offer Mr. Ellis the same premium as Tischer, 11%, and not one penny more. That was audacious. Ellis must have learned by now that Tischer had been paid and that his jewels were the only ones still at large--thus, they were more valuable just by the basic law of supply and demand. But my orders were firm. No bargaining.

Once at the Cavendish hotel in London, I was handed a message from a Mrs. Ann Ellis, maybe a relative of the diamond dealer, requesting me to call her. Exhausted from my early-morning trip, I decided to have breakfast first and business later. On my way to the coffee shop, a bellboy was roaming the lobby holding a sign with my name scribbled on it. Strangely enough, a man walked up to the bellboy, introduced himself, and took the message that was destined for me. I decided to observe the usurper's moves. He quickly reviewed the written note and burst out of the hotel to get a mode of transportation, I assumed. Sure enough, his car was parked outside. I would not mind if we would switch identities as long as we switched cars. He can take my VW Golf and me his DB5 (that is Aston Martin for the uninitiated who think the world of their Honda Civic). I snapped into action, hailed a cab and without sounding too mysterious or funny told the cabby: "Follow that car."

We drove for only a few short minutes before arriving at the Royal Automobile Club in Pall Mall. I saw the falsifier of identities walking into the Club's main reception hall. There the reception-ist directed him toward a table where a handsome, well-groomed, perfectly attired, fifty-something man was waiting for him. The gentleman looked like some sort of a diplomat or a member of the House of Lords. I could tell that he was not part of any funny business, unlike my impersonator. Something in this man's face oozed serenity, and his demeanor was one of natural confidence. I had no business to attend to, and my agitation was becoming suspicious to the snobbish, empire-styled valets of the RAC. I decided to discreetly wait outside. A few minutes later, while enduring London's depressing weather, my impersonator emerged alone. The valet brought up his car and he jumped behind the wheel. I followed him on foot, being certain that he would go back to my hotel! By simply calling my room and getting no reply, he could figure out whether I was in or still out. Sure enough, when I arrived breathless in my room, the phone was ringing off the hook. Deliberately, I did not pick up, just to keep the ploy going. I hid behind the curtains, with the table lamp in my hand, and waited.

Moments later, I heard a knock on my door, which started my adrenaline rush. The door opened slowly; a man had peeked his head when my lamp, with its fifteen pounds of ebony wood, greeted him with a welcoming frontal blow. The mystery man fell unconscious. When he woke up, I had tied him to a chair using my invaluable horseback riding kit that included, among other things, a harness with a rope that would hold steady a Holsteiner Stallion in full heat (don't bother asking; I am through with explaining every detail in this book, and frankly I am tired of your lack of culture, which you have demonstrated beyond a doubt by simply purchasing a copy of this book in the first place!). I had gagged his mouth with a small towel that I drenched with a cocktail of Fernet Branca and Tabasco sauce, all wonders of the Mini Bar. He looked like a young clerk with short hair, and eyes that expressed not even the slightest sign of intelligence.

When he regained his senses, I introduced myself. He could not reciprocate with the drenched cloth stuffed down his throat. I had no experience in the field of physical torture, so I had to indulge in some mental games to get him to spit out (literally) the reason behind his bad act. I dragged him into the bathroom and pushed him toward the bathtub. I turned the tap, and started filling the bath. I then brought the "welcome lamp," plugged it in the wall, grabbed its ebony handle and watched the naked wires of the broken light glow. For a moment his eyes shifted into watermelons. In a swift move I dipped the lamp into the bathtub, igniting an electrical current of the kind you'd rather not experiment with on any part of your anatomy, hard or soft. Having finished with the demo, I turned to my muzzled "chair person," and lamp in hand, started pushing him forward. At that moment, the cloth in his mouth shrank as he started to choke on it while desperately trying to say something. He seemed perplexed about the torture technique I was saving for him. Was he supposed to suffocate from the spiced gag, or be electrocuted? His eyes were his only mode of communication. If eyes could only speak was an understatement. He looked helpless. He looked pale. He looked like he was not ready to get into hot water yet.

I violently tilted back his chair forcing him to fall, and proceeded with my inquisition. I stood on top of him with my shoes well dug in, and started my questioning. I told him to answer with yes (two nods) or no (one nod). Was he sent by Ellis? Why did he impersonate me, and how did he know I was coming to London? Who was the man he met at my expense at the RAC? All these questions--and no answers from my mothballed alter ego. I finally brought my self to remove the filthy cloth, using gloves. Still no words. The man had turned mute. He could not speak properly. His lips were swollen beyond belief. I quickly made a mental note to nickname him "Rubber Lips." I did not feel sorry for this son of a bitch who had just played me. After he gasped for air, and gained some comfort, he gave away his mission. Even the smallest details were not spared. He was simply the chauffeur of Mr. Ellis, the diamond dealer, charged with following me around town. He got excited at the idea of doing more than his daily routine (i.e., walking the dog or dogging the maid, I presume) and decided to get into his "James Bond" role. Driving the boss' car must have given him some illusions. (The Aston Martin was not for this bloke. Thank goodness. There was justice in the world). The man he had met at the RAC was named Ramsay Sacks. He apparently extended an invitation to me (not my impersonator) to his suite at the Dorchester, the next day. He apparently was high up at Inter-Finance. I had never heard of him before.

I gave him leave, but kept the car keys after having jotted down the address of Mr. Ellis, where I was expected at 8:30 p.m. sharp. The call from a Mrs. Ellis was for the same invite. I took my long-awaited shower, shaved, put on my smart black suit, and headed to some part of Belgravia looking for a Victorian house that belonged to a modern-day diamond dealer. Driving the Aston Martin was not only a pleasure, but on this occasion it was an out-of-body experience. I was sure that the chauffeur did not tell his employer that he left more than just some feathers on the battlefield. He left a rare bird, which I very much enjoyed flying, indeed. I parked the car and proceeded to the main gate when I noticed a car sitting on the opposite side of the street. But when I saw its occupants, I felt less nervous. They looked like a security detail from Scotland Yard. Hats off, windows rolled up, one was stuffing a pipe and the other reading the morning papers. The chairman must have alerted them in order to put extra pressure on Ellis, I figured. Knowing their keen interest in solving mysteries, they surely obliged.

The door opened and a forty-something beauty appeared. Her elegant black dress was matched by her refined hands. She had brown eyes that had a hypnotic effect, sandy-blonde hair, a body to retireb for (or into), and a smile that motivated high crimes and grave misdemeanors. "You must be our foreign guest? Hi, I am Ann, Mrs. Ellis."

"Precisely," I replied while kissing her gentle hand. It is always refreshing, once in Anglia, to be subtly reminded of your alien origins. The gentle lady did not sound disrespectful, but rather simply deprecating, as if I had been invited to be showcased. I proceeded into the foyer and gave the butler (Jeeves, I suppose?) the keys to the Aston Martin. Neither the butler nor her Ladyship Ann of Belgravia looked one bit surprised. I thought by now they must have known that the gaffer-chauffeur had failed in his clandestine mission. I was ushered into a smoking lounge with Old Masters hanging from the walls, and the usual paraphernalia that distinguishes Anglo-Saxon "salons" from Latin ones. See, in Paris or Rome the living rooms would be well-lit, the air flowing, art books on the coffee table, classical music playing in the background, and one painting –usually a still nature or landscape--hanging in the middle wall. In Anglo-Saxon abodes, the lights are dim, the fireplace ablaze–even in summer time, unknown art works –usually sad or fear-inspiring portraits--haunt the walls, and the only sound is that of damp silence. It's more than just a difference in lifestyle…it's a whole difference in attitude. Mr. Ellis looked like Nathan Meyer Rothschild in his famous illustration at the London Stock Exchange: short, round-bellied, wide eyes glowing with mischief. He greeted me with borrowed warmth and a fake smile. He introduced me to his guests: Mr. and Mrs. Dixon, attorneys at law; Dr. Harriman, ecologist; and Mrs. Leeson, some rich divorcée in quest of a new coffer to rob, I guess. The chit-chat was on botanicals, with Dr. Harriman recounting his latest trip to India. When a Brit pronounces the word "India" you can sense the angst in his voice for having lost the Great Empire and all. I learned about all sorts of exotic plants, of migrating birds, of mosquitoes that liked plants but disliked birds, of birds that hated some kind of plants but absolutely ravished some mosqui-toes, and so on.... At dinner I was seated between our hostess and the divorcée, who plunged into her drinks in an attempt to find the depth of her soul.

Shortly after dinner, Barry Ellis respectfully took leave of his guests and invited me to follow him to the study. He went straight to the point, gave me his Swiss Bank transfer details, and asked me to wire the money with a 100% premium within 48 hours. Both he and I knew that he was in a position to ask for even more while holding a bit longer onto the rocks. My instructions were limited to an 11% markup, I said. He just went ballistic! He could ask for a 500% premium and InterFinance could do zilch about it! He was doing us a favor, he was letting us go with honor, and he wanted his 100% markup, basta! I promised to call him the next morning after talking to my principals.

On my way out he asserted to me that the certificates were genu-ine...the only question I was trusted to ask. He dealt in no fakes, he asserted. I thought he had no reason to associate himself with criminals of the lowest order when he himself enjoyed the high-est ranking in the Royal Order of Thievery (I just made that one up although it truly exists in England and its is called the guild of

City Bankers). That would be going down market for him, which judging from his taste in "Nature Morte" paintings and "Living Nature" possessions, he was not about to do any time soon. He happened to get his hands on some "hot rocks" that were legit and wanted to cash on such a unique opportunity.

I was walking out of the front portal when the Lady Ann of Belgravia whispered in my ear to head straight to the "club" in Mayfair and wait for her. She said to give them the password "hot mate" at the door in order to be let in. It was a good hour before Ann showed up at the Ccub dressed in a short dress and long heels. After exchanging passionate kisses, we had few single malts, many laughs, and a number of intimate moments, before we waltzed our way back to her apartment in Chelsea. Ann, as she put it, was "completely off" her husband, with whom she had no Biblical rapport since Moses last crossed the sea. Pardon my perverted mind, but a picture came to mind at that particular moment: the Red Sea opening up at the command of Moses' stick, leading the way to the Promised Land. Ann was gracious in her moves, gentle with her hands, soft with her voice, and engaging all over. No dirty words, no tricks, no cuffs or kinky stuff. Just an old-fashioned beauty, a lady-like creature. The kind Princess D would come to represent many years later. You can tell a lady not by her table manners or her public behavior, but by her lingerie. I know that you have in mind the cheap Victoria's Secrets catalogue. Forget it. This was pure silk from La Perla and real stockings from Dior, not to mention the slippers from Sidoni Larizzi. This woman was worthy of a king, and yet she was married to a thug in suit. I could tell that she wanted to avoid any discussions about him, any reference to the dinner or to the after-dinner chat, like we had just met at the club without previous history. With a genuine gem like Ann, who needed stolen diamonds? Not me, surely. Our passionate moment was punctuated by brief telling silences, looking gently at each other. She was a balsam to the heart, and much more--a cure that I was intending to take in little doses, without prescription, and hopefully with a lot of side effects. All her sides gave me the same effect: never wanting to stop or reconsider. We decided after hours of love-making to take a soothing bath and to catch some sleep. That was a wise decision that permitted me to discover that Ann was not only a princess, but a mermaid too.

I returned to my hotel room in the morning only to find an urgent telegram at the reception desk. The moment I opened it I felt a severe migraine. Rutger Zarmat's Falcon Jet had vanished over the Atlantic on his return from New York. The news was devastating. Was he dead? Was it sabotage? Murder? I was shocked. What struck me in the message was that Mrs. Gotryne had written it with a *post-scriptum* that felt more like a *post-mortem*: "Please get in touch immediately with Mr. Ramsay Sacks at the Dorchester Hotel in London in his capacity as interim chairman!" So soon was a replacement found...and of all people, it was the very same person I was supposed to meet for breakfast. Coincidence was on sale today! I snatched a copy of the *FT* and there it was, on the second page. The virtual obituary of Rutger Zarmat, the man who brought me into all this, and to whom I could not pay my last respects. Was there any reason to all this? Was I getting sentimental? That was the scary part...having to discover that I had a heart. False alarm! I ran into my room, took a quick shower and headed straight to the Dorchester to meet the new man in charge of Inter-Finance. The chairman is dead; long live the chairman!

Sacks received me in his suite and presented his sympathies for the disappearance of Zarmat. I found that extremely gallant of him. He must have known Rutger Zarmat for over three decades at least, and here he was giving me words of comfort. Some people steal your mind with gold bullion, others with a gun, some with words--but with Sacks it was subtle touches. An eloquent, old school financier who despised current-day merchants and traders, he was amused by the episode at the RAC and even asked whether the masquerading driver survived the ploy. He had my photo on him, delivered by courier from Inter-Finance. When he saw the driver at the club, he immediately knew that something must have gone wrong–but nothing serious, he hoped. Then things got more serious. The newly anointed chairman–now alive and kicking until further notice--inquired about my negotiations with Ellis. He was disgusted, but not the least surprised at the ransom that the diamond merchant wanted to extort. He instructed me to call a certain Georges Selleck, a special security expert at Inter-Finance. He had some interesting data to share. I was to report back to Sacks in the evening.

I ran out of the hotel and headed straight to Selleck's office on Fleet Street. Selleck was a legend in his own right: a veteran of the French Foreign Legion, the SAS, and for a long time an esteemed collaborator of the CIA. Selleck was expecting me in his dungeon-like office. He was sitting on one side of his desk, hand stretched out for a manly salute. "The chairman gave me instructions to give you all the stuff we've got on Ellis, and here it is." He opened a brown file that contained ten nude pictures with Barry Ellis practicing sodomy with teenage boys in various positions! The direct result of public school education in Britain, I suppose. Imagine the scene: boys sleeping next to boys, in dark corridors, during endless rainy nights in the English countryside. Going solo with a nudie magazine in the confines of some smelly toilet must become boring and less pleasurable, after a while.

Back to the present, I asked Georges what I could do with said photos and he replied, "Show them to his lady--she will hate him and love you more." Failing to reply to his insinuation that I had spent the night with this pedophile's wife. I immediately replied that giving her the pictures was of no use if getting the diamonds were our goal, rather than a marital scandal. The well-dressed corporate gorilla agreed with a simple nod. He was instructed by Sacks to keep an eye on me in London. Things were getting edgy after Zarmat's disappearance.

Shortly after, we stormed into Barry Ellis's office, closed the door, cut the phone cable, and confined him to his chair. I then threw the photos on the desk. His heart started beating at high speed, his eyes were the size of golf balls, and he was about to burst into tears. "Our gems for yours," I said, "or these photos will be plastered all over the diamond districts around the world, from 48th Street in New York, to Antwerp to Tel Aviv and back to London."

Ellis was jumpy, knocking his head against the mahogany desk in a clear sign of despair. The refined art collector, married to a charming lady, an entertainer of distinguished guests, running a flourishing diamond business, was now reduced to a mere sexual pervert. Talk about a reversal of fortune, in a snapshot, literally. He must have cursed all photographic discoveries. The early cameras, the Polaroid, the videos, the camcorders and all the equipment that could register with high definition bodily be-haviors at intimate moments. As if a spell had been lifted, Ellis's tongue was liberated and he demanded that we hand over all pho-tos and negatives in exchange for giving up the stones. We agreed and he, in a simple move, emptied his pockets! They were on him all the time. He also handed over the certificates that were issued by NeraGem. We took the goods, I grabbed the certificates, paid him the money (including the 11% premium), and Selleck took the papers to the forensic lab.

I was back at the Dorchester's apartment-suite, where the current chairman lived all year round, surrounded by his Berber servants. He had brought them back from his native Egypt after Nasser had the idea of regaining control of Suez Canal, kicking out the Brits for good. Nasser added to the grandiose Canal constructed by De Lesseps a hideous dam built by the Soviets. They surely had demonstrated their wall-building quality in Berlin. Ramsay's family belonged to the aristocracy of pre-Revolutionary Egypt, something incomparable with the rags of today. Nothing is, really. His family, I was told later, lived a very different life in a different world and lived like kings, with cotton farms, sugar cane plantations, textile factories. They dealt in bullion, sold timber, imported coal, and controlled commerce. Back to the present time, the chairman was very happy with the progress made so far. The diamonds were back in our possession, and we had the opportunity to analyze the certificates more closely. The chairman instructed Selleck and me to go to Sierra Leone and find out the origin of this mess. Without delay, we boarded the company's private jet to Sierra Leone, leaving at 2 a.m., which gave me sufficient time to see Ann again, and for Selleck to get the lab results.

I did not know what to tell Ann. This hesitation was not stimulated by decency, but by the fear of her reaction and the stronger attachment she would have toward me. Do not get me wrong; I liked Ann, but not in a serious manner. What was I supposed to do? I finally decided to tell her, only to be shocked that she knew it all along. Ann was not a bit surprised. She reacted with calm and indifference. That really lifted a weight off my shoulders.

Our encounter was not less surprising, though, as we indulged in moments of extreme intimacy filled with passionate embraces. I left while she was still asleep and went straight to my hotel where Selleck & Co. were waiting for me to rush to the airport. Georges had the lab results and he was cross because nothing in said certificates had any trace of forgery. We decided to give it a rest and to tackle the issue first thing in the morning upon arrival.

General Abdo Dibondieu was waiting for us at the tarmac, dressed in his Idi Amin outfit and surrounded by a battalion of soldiers perched on Jeeps and ready for battle. I advanced to shake his hand and he instead grabbed me in a bear hug that almost exhausted all the oxygen from my body. What an overwhelming display of affection, I thought. We boarded his armored Range Rover and we headed toward NeraGem's offices. In the car we discussed the rescue operation in London and the enigma of the near authentic certificates. General Abdo Dibondieu seemed adamant about forgery and about the fact that such certificates were falsified somewhere in Europe, slapped onto our gems and then resold as "legit" rocks. In short he saw no reason for us coming to Sierra Leone, because the falsifications were being perpetrated in some sophisticated print shop in Munich or London. He nonetheless welcomed our trip for maybe we could dig up something he might have missed. *Yeah, right*, I thought. All this rumbling about focusing on Europe rather than Sierra Leone made me uncomfortable. I detected the same malaise in Selleck's eyes, who was no fool and had met (and slaughtered) many a general in his career.

Security at NeraGem's compound was airtight. The compound was guarded 24/7 by paramilitary troops whose loyalty was to NeraGem. There were secured gates, sniffing dogs, high-tech alarms, ditches, bunkers, semi-heavy automatic weapons at each entrance and exit, metal detectors, gem detectors, and round-the-clock CCTVs that recorded all moves in and out of the facilities. The mines produced the diamonds and the office issued the certificates. Ironically, the certificates were more important for us at this stage then the rocks.

The certificates were issued and signed by Becker Vig, the CEO of NeraGem, a company man whose reputation and credibility were beyond reproach. They were also adorned with the government's seal, which was affixed and signed by pre-designated officials. No reason for them to cheat, since they would be defrauding themselves of revenues. We did not display the certificates that we brought back from London, and instead requested to see a sample certificate already issued for an existing lot. The resemblance was striking. It seemed like a dead end. After hours of deliberations we excused ourselves, went straight to our bungalows, and agreed to meet later for drinks around the pool.

Back in the bungalow I took out the London certificates and compared them with the ones I had just seen in the office. They were all signed identically: "Exchequer of Sierra Leone." However, on the ones in my hand the "E" in Exchequer was twisted, and so was the "S" in Sierra. Selleck came into my room with a list of the authorized representatives who could sign on behalf of the government: two Treasury officials, and...guess who? General DiBondieu. The trouble was that DiBondieu had been trusted for twenty years and had no reason--financial or moral--to betray NeraGem. We had no clues, so we decided to catch up with some sleep before the evening party.

The African music woke me up. I headed toward the pool after a quick shower and a change of wardrobe. The barbecue had already started. The food was being readied with a mixture of spices that stirred (but did not shake) my appetite. Alcohol was flowing in the guests' cups, and some were dancing. The sky was clear, and a breeze of warm air was filling the surroundings, with leaves cracking a gentle, natural music. All the senior management of NeraGem was present, and Becker introduced me to each one of them. At the bar, an old but well-trained waiter was working the bottles, mixing all sorts of alcohol with fresh juices. He insisted that I try the "Antelope" shot, which was made of whiskey, banana juice, hot peppers, lemon soda, and cola. The secret was to keep the drinks at all times in an icebox. That recipe had worked wonders with Gen. DiBondieu, Hassan the bar-man assured me. The general had even requested a full bottle of "Antelope" to be put in an ice-filled bucket and flown with him on his latest trip to Geneva. Hassan waited on him in NerGem's private plane during that trip.

"So, Hassan" I said "how did you manage to bring enough ice cubes on the private jet which has a small mini bar." (Remember I had flown that plane into Sierra Leone twelve hours ago, for those of you whose memory is failing you.)

Hassan retorted, "No need, sir; one icebox suffices. I swear, sir, the general had his own airtight icebox and the ice cubes did not even melt." Maybe it's the pepper in the drinks?

Back to the party, I spotted Becker talking to a young African lady: Nawinda, who worked as a chief gemologist at the plant. She had studied at the prestigious Santa Monica School of Gemology in L.A. and was a first-rate gem grader. One more tip--she was Becker Vig's adopted child. Naturally, she knew nothing about my role, and Becker hurried to introduce me as the young advisor of the group on a routine trip to inspect compliance manuals. I was interested in talking to her more about diamonds. We chatted and joked about the reason why women worshiped diamonds. Nawinda's theory was pretty simple. She insisted that women liked diamonds because unlike with men, size did not matter; only purity. Wow! What a way to provoke me, but I did not react. I looked confused for the first time that evening, and I even detected her joy at putting me in an uncomfortable position. I uttered some incomprehensible words, and went looking for Selleck for moral support. I found Georges with Becker debating the question of Dibondieu's loyalty. Becker was furious that we even thought about, let alone questioned the general's morality. The general had fought with rebel forces around the mines for over fifteen years, losing comrades in combat, witnessed civilians being slaughtered, and all this in defense of our interests. He was the most dependable ally for NeraGem according to Becker, and we had no reason (and apparently no right) to put his loyalty to the test. We left it there and headed to the large dinner table. I was seated next to a couple of engineers who worked in the mines. They belabored to explain the intricate process of mining the rocks from down under.

After dinner, I asked Nawinda to brief me on the mines of NeraGem and on the diamonds trade in Sierra Leone, in general. She obliged. It seems that in Sierra Leone, and to my great surprise, there were two mining regions and hence two concessions. One active, NeraGem, and another out of service called BiancaGem. So much for creativity and corporate branding! The BiancaGem concession was operated prior to the civil war by a German mining group who had to stop all activities due to the repeated incursions of guerilla forces and counter-attacks by the regulars, led by no one else than General DiBondieu. The guerrilla forces were almost closing in on the mine when the German group decided to detonate a large quantity of explosives and block the entrance, but not before they had, in the middle of the night, dismantled all the mining equipment and transported it to the other side. Our side, that is. Zarmat, having been tipped by Becker Vig, arranged to purchase all the equipment at a hefty premium. In effect, he dismantled the competition. Nawinda knew all of these details from her father. She went on, telling me that the Germans had used the services of Georges Selleck to properly implode the gates of the BiancaGem mines and seal it for good. NeraGem became a monopoly overnight and the government had cut off the rebels' funding sources. Whoever said that public-private partnership did not work?

Now I started to realize the close relationship between the interests of the local government and our company, and why Selleck was on board for this mission. The only dupe so far had been me. Why had they brought me into this mess? I knew nothing about diamonds and after Nawinda's description of their perception by women, I cared less for them than when I first started. So the rebels had no money and no resources, but they continued to fight? How did they take care of their people, their families? As far as immediate humanitarian relief was concerned, a monastery of Franciscan friars had been in the region since the early 1900s. The monastery was located in today's "No Man's Land" between the rebels' positions and government troops. The friars were given a safe passage between both camps. They ran a hospital, an orphanage, and a school for children. In fact, Nawinda had been raised in that orphanage until the age of three when Becker expressed his wishes to the friars to adopt a girl, and by the second week, Nawinda was sleeping in the company's compound. The friars visited both sides, took care of the wounded in times of skirmishes, and held prayers for the dead after giving them a proper burial service. It worked in that peculiar way for many years and all sides were happy with this arrangement. I bid Nawinda good night and headed to my room, where I wanted to have a serious talk with Georges Selleck.

"You did not ask about BiancaGem!" was Georges' reply. "In my business we do not tell bedtime stories to strangers!" With my face lit by rage, I told him with a voluminous tone that, while he might be a legend in his own right, and that while he may have beheaded many gorillas in the mist and blown some mines on the way over, I was in charge of this mission (don't ask me why). And the next time I discovered a new story connecting him to this enigma, I would gladly make sure that he ended up his career with Inter-Finance, as a parking guard in downtown Karachi! My speech worked wonders. Georges did not respond to fear, greed, or threat of imminent danger, but only to authority. We continued our chat on this basis. His intelligence sources informed him of some mysterious happenings close to our mine. One thing in particular seemed to bother him: 9 mm caliber bullets. I had no clue what he was mumbling about. Well, our guards used Heckler & Koch MP5 machine guns. Their usage was strictly restricted, no shipment from the factory in Germany, whether legal or illegal reached Sierra Leone if not destined to NeraGem. The government did not even have access to them. The rebels had no use of this type of ammo, since they fired Russian-made AK47s. The AK47s were effective, but heavy, and not very useful in close protection missions. NeraGem made sure to have at all times sufficient quantities of 9 mm ammo, used in the MP5s. A large stock of it was stolen in recent past. That was in the past three months coinciding with the time of the diamonds' forgery. Was there any connection between these events? His question was addressed to me, the supposed smart ass in charge of the mission.

"We will go tomorrow and find out," I said. To tell you the truth, I felt comfortable in this man's company--not only in the jungles of Sierra Leone, but even in the confines of a boardroom. Compared with lawyers he had ethics, his own Code of War. Compared with bankers, he had guts and asked for no collateral to put his assets in harm's way.

I decided to call Sacks on a secured line to get his approval for the trip and to obtain the required security passes and authorizations. It was almost midnight in London, and Sacks's voice was as fresh as sunrise. He approved of my move and asked me to check out the friars' convent. I jokingly asked if he had any particular confession to convey to the superior. He replied in a cold voice that betrayed a warning, "No, not really, just beware of Judas." That did not help me gain any comfort. I stayed up all night mulling his words and anticipating next morning's events.

The trip to the NeraGem mines took over three hours by car. We left around 4:00 a.m. in an armored convoy accompanied by Selleck's legionnaires and an army detachment that escorted Gen. DibonDieu almost everywhere. I dozed off in the car. When I woke up, the sights and sounds of the African plain were simply too beautiful to miss. The vegetation was lush, the air was filled with currents of warm breezes, and the sun was in a blazing splendor. No photo safari can ever capture majestic Africa. Think about it, how could anyone bottle the ocean? Impossible, right? Made my point. (You don't have to thank me for this brilliant comparison, but next time you use it in the boardroom, tearoom, or any other settings where you will try to impress others, do bother to quote me!) I felt no sympathy for those sorry-ass travel agents and promoters of jungle voyages; those overpaid and underdressed National Geographic buffoons, along with all camera makers, film developers, and chroniclers of tropical trips who might as well zip it for good and get lost. You cannot capture the plain with a zoom.

We tagged along in the convoy and left conversations to a minimum until we reached our final destination. The security chief at the mine was a chap called Troy Laz--an ex-convict, I presumed, by the serial number on his wrist. He was the living proof of Darwin's theory. (Okay, enough monkey talk for now, ha ha). The main gates of NeraGem's mine were heavily guarded with armed men whose arsenal included M-60 heavy machine guns mounted on Jeeps, RPG shoulder missiles, and the infamous MP5 machine guns. After few niceties, we agreed to take a little pause and to reassemble within an hour in Troy's operations room to assess the security data. Once inside the bunker-like camp, I felt as if I were in a first- class industrial facility with no signs of tension, security concerns, or unnerving behavior. All personnel wore a tag that clearly stated his/her name, title, security code, and photo. The mines had their entrances located at the backend of the camp. Surveillance systems were in place, both inside and outside the facility, with control towers at each corner dominating all surrounding areas.

Changed but not shaved, I reached the operations room to find everyone present. Troy started to update us on the latest surveillance findings including, minor rebel incursions South West of the camp, the discovery of 9 mm cartridges in the bushes, which explained the use of the stolen ammo from our storage. There also was one more detail. The addition, in the past months, of one new member to the Franciscans' congregation. Nothing too alarming so far. Troy had ordered breakfast for all. Having lived under British rules, our host had two choices for breakfast: bacon and eggs, or nothing. I always preferred the second choice, but decided to do the healthy thing, which was asking for egg whites without the bacon. It is then that I precisely heard the most interesting clue of the day: "You're doing like the new friar," said Troy.

"And what's that?" I inquired innocently.

"Going kosher!" Supposedly, when the new Franciscan checked into our facility on a courtesy visit, Troy, in a rare gesture of good manners, offered him some fresh bacon supplies, which the friar declined, and snapping at Troy he told him that bacon was forbidden. Forbidden? To whom and by whom? Not Jesus, last I checked. The friar could have said that bacon was not good for one's cholesterol level as prescribed by the surgeon general, and that would fine by me. But forbidden? That was too strong a word. (Now, in your great minds you must have thought that I was making too big a deal about this. That while friars were not allowed to have sex with altar boys, they at least should be perfectly free to limit the intake of fat into their bodies. Yes, but we are not discussing Dr. Atkins in my book and the level of saturated fats are no concerns of mine. This book is a serie noire novel that hunts for clues about mysteries and you are becoming my bête noire for having no clues at all).

I stood up and asked Troy to take me immediately to the North Tower that overlooks the monastery. Georges, sensing an emergency by instinct (unlike my readers, whose good instinct to purchase this book was a sign of their debatable intelligence), jumped from the table, took his binoculars and followed us. The general thought that something important was happening, but not more important than his food. His priorities that morning gave him the nickname I have been looking for throughout this chapter: General Food. Admit it, it is becoming.

Once in the North Tower, I asked if Troy could point out the new friar. Troy called one of the sentinels who regularly surveyed the monastery, including the friars' daily habits (we will not go into this one). The sentinel took his own binoculars and searched the horizon for his target. "There he is," he shouted, "trimming the bushes around the lodgings." I grabbed Georges' pair of long-view binoculars, and followed the voice and the hand instructions of the sentinel to locate the priest. When my sights were finally set on him, with the 20/20 vision enhancement lenses of my military-grade binoculars, my heart almost missed a beat. I immediately knew why Sacks uttered the word Judas, why I was sent over here, and even why the 9 mm bullets were being depleted! But with all this, the puzzle was getting thicker, far-reaching, and somewhat more complicated than ever.

I must have frozen for few seconds, because when I came back to my senses, Georges was almost shouting in my ear: "Who the hell is he? Do you know him? Does this have anything to do with our mysterious diamonds?"

I lowered the binoculars and with a voice that was hardly coming out of my already dehydrated mouth, I answered, "Definitely-- but how, I don't know yet!"

We returned to the operations room, and as if the world depended on my lips, I informed my impatient audience that the new friar was no other than Col. Yoram Mirador of the Israeli

Mossad. Silence fell in the room with a thud, like the Japs on Pearl Harbor. I did not dwell on the recent events of Spain, but asked them to take my word for granted that he must have been behind the smuggling of diamonds, the network of rogue dealers in Amsterdam and London, and the probable traffic of Israeli-manufactured Uzis, which use 9 mm caliber. That much I knew by instinct. Yoram must have set up an arms deal with the rebels and encouraged them to finance it locally through the sale of diamonds!

"What diamonds?" shouted General Food. "We have full control of the stock of diamonds of Sierra Leone."

"Well, it might be that our monopoly days are over," I retorted. "It was possible," I replied, "for IDF's corps of engineers to have devised a means to regain access to the depth of the BiancaGem's mines."

General Food looked whiter than South Africa's Apartheid regime. He did not suspect me of knowing this historical fact. "No way!" he shouted back at me with anger, "that mine is gone, and Georges knows it better than anyone."

The ever-cautious mercenary said that while re-opening the tunnels that he'd helped blow up some years ago would be very difficult, it was not totally impossible. My theory was holding on firm ground. The theory was plausible. The Israelis helped the rebels dig the mines to enrich their leaders, finance the civil war, and fund part of Mossad's black-ops in Africa. The rebels smuggled the "ice" into the market by using NeraGem's certificates of origin; they pocketed the proceeds and paid the Yids for their services. "Hot diamonds" were sold legitimately on the international market. The inventory of NeraGem's rocks remained untouched, and if and when NeraGem's principals ever found out, they would keep their mouths shut or risk destroying their brand equity. It was simple. Better still, it was brilliant!

However, more clues remained missing. First, somebody at NeraGem–not on the outside, as General Food had assured us--was actively assisting the rebels with the paper forgery. Second, that someone must have devised the perfect means of carrying the diamonds out of Sierra Leone, bypassing our airtight security. Finally, for the ruthless rebels to remit the white rocks and collect the greenbacks, they must have trusted a person whose loyalty was beyond the shadow of a doubt. This conundrum was too complex. That mystery person must have been a high-level insider of NeraGem, while at the same time, carrying favors for the rebels?!

I was restless, and while I was thinking about the maze of this criminal plot, Georges came into my room to read my mind on this one. I drew a total blank. Really, when I felt I was getting close, this matter sank like the Titanic before my eyes. I decided to go to the north tower to monitor the movements in the monastery. It was almost 6:00 p.m. and the sun was starting its hide-and-seek routine with the moon. I got into the surveillance room of the tower and put on a headset for night vision. All was green. All was quiet. For a good while nothing moved, and I stayed on for nearly two hours, when at around 7:50 p.m., I spotted a woman, dressed in white, and seemingly undeterred by the security system surrounding the camp, who was coming from the direction of the monastery toward our main gate.

"Who is that lady" I asked the sentinel.

"Oh, that is Fatima, the local dialect teacher at the Franciscans' school; she visits regularly and takes provisions for her younger students."

I remembered Nawinda telling me about her days at the monastery school. I resumed my professional voyeur mission. Another hour had passed when Georges, who did not initially follow me to the tower, emerged from the stairwell, obviously disturbed. He asked me to follow him at once. I obliged. Georges, as it turned out, had installed eavesdropping devices in General Food's room, just in case. He went on to tell me that during the past thirty minutes, the general had been sobbing in his room as if death's messenger had visited him with a signed and sealed package. Something grave must have happened.

I decided to act. I was determined to confront General Food, 'cause I suspected he knew more than he claimed. I did not even bother to knock, and when I opened the door I saw Fatima the teacher, kneeling at the general's feet, crying in silence while the general was obviously shattered and distraught. "General, is everything all right?" I asked. I was not really expecting an answer, but a reaction. The general remained calm while the teacher stood up, while covering her head with a scarf. She was not particularly disturbed by my presence, so I immediately discounted the possibility of having stepped into a lovers' scene. It was more serious, definitely. "So, General," I added, "could we talk in private?" The general, whose cheeks were brightly painted with fresh tears, and whose fixated eyes told stories of miserable endings, looked up at me and with his hand gestured to close the door. I shut the door and took a seat.

"He's got my boy," the general uttered. "He's got our boy," he quickly corrected himself while looking sadly upon Fatima. I was waiting for the rest of the story and it came with no delay.

Some years ago, the rebels had killed Fatima's husband, who worked as a gardener at the monastery. They suspected him of spying for the regulars, and specifically for General Food. It did not help that the general, who was fond of Fatima, used to regularly invite both husband and wife to dinners at the camp. In fact, General Food was Fatima's secret lover and felt responsible for her husband's death. Moreover, at the time of the crime, Fatima was pregnant with the general's baby. The general was married and they had to keep up appearances. So, after the baby was born, he was raised by his legitimate mother at the orphans' school at the nearby monastery. During all this time, the natural father kept a close watch on his bastard from the nearby camp--until some three months ago, when the new Friar John, aka Yoram, insisted on meeting Fatima.

Arriving at her abode located near the school, the new friar, accompanied by another man, snatched the boy and entrusted him to his companion. He had never been seen since. Yoram instructed Fatima to make contact with General Food and to arrange for a meeting. He obviously knew about their affair. In the meantime, the boy was held hostage. Having been alerted, General Food quickly arranged to meet Yoram. At the meeting, Yoram blackmailed the general (as you should by now have suspected, if the hamster in your head has not fallen asleep at the wheel!) to conduct the diamond-laundering scheme along the lines I had deciphered few hours earlier. Yoram had threatened to kill the boy if the general betrayed him. General Food's killer instinct prevailed upon him at this encounter as he tried to cut Yoram's throat there and then, only to find out (as I sadly did in Spain) that Yoram was a knife expert. He wrestled with the general's arm and ended up inflicting serious wounds in two of his right-hand fingers…which explained the twisted signatures on the forged certificates of origin and the "bear hugs" the general insisted on, avoiding all handshakes.

It was left to the general to smuggle the "hot" diamonds. The rocks were initially brought into the camp by Fatima. The general, in turn, emptied the "ice" into the bucket that kept the "Antelope" shot cool during the trip from Sierra Leone to Geneva. That kind of ice naturally does not melt! At arrival, the diamonds were safely handed over to dealers in Europe with a genuinely signed certificate. The general had no intention of playing games with his son's abductors. He even felt somewhat relieved that he was not really stealing from NeraGem, but was simply "floating" somebody else's merchandise under our brand name. Poor bastard. I had judged him too harshly. Here he was in tears and desperate. The reason for his despair, as I figured out, was that Yoram had effectively enslaved him for life. That I could not bear. That would not happen on my watch, at least not twice. Yoram and the scheme of hot diamonds had to be stopped for good, and I was resolute in seeing that through.

The general told me that a rendezvous with Yoram was agreed to take place at 2:00 a.m. this very morning. The general was expected to hand over the proceeds from the diamond sale to the rebel leader, Jonas Macabreto, at the former site of BiancaGem's mine. The general's meeting with Yoram was to show proof of proceeds, and for General Food to obtain the release of his boy into his mother's custody at the monastery. Yoram's men, to dissuade Fatima from any foolish attempt to smuggle the boy, would surround the monastery. After the stopover at the monastery, the general, accompanied by Yoram, would make the journey to the mine to hook up with Jonas, deliver the money, and get new rocks to sell. It was time to call Georges and to give him my instructions. I did not even check with Sacks on the details of my plan, in order to avoid any last-minute pullouts. This was my war, not theirs, and I wanted to fight the only way the likes of Yoram understood it: dirty. So we made our preparations, and the general moved across the demarcation lines and pressed on to the monastery. It was almost 2:05 a.m. and I could see, from the height of the northern tower, Yoram frisking the general in search of weapons and opening up the sports bag that carried the $15 million. All went as planned, and by 2:11 a.m. they were on their way to the other mine. Fatima was in the school with her boy, encircled by Yoram's mini army. Success depended on one issue: honor. Was General Food going to behave as the honorable warrior he once was? I had no doubts. Before he departed, I wished him goodbye and he finally shook my hand for the first time. I knew too well what that meant.

The old gates of BiancaGem's mine were still closed by rubbles from Selleck's last blast, but the Israeli corps of engineers had opened a smart ditch on top of the hill using very sophisticated tunnel-digging machinery. From that small bore, young boys lowered their frail bodies down a chute of almost 150 meters deep, clinging to ropes and armed with mine lamps in search of some rocks. The Jeep carrying the general came to a full stop at the mine's entrance. Yoram came out first and Jonas, the rebel leader, approached to savor his victory over the proud general. The general opened his door, lifted his body, walked toward them with a smile, and while thinking of his boy and the salvation of his soul, detonated the explosive belt that Selleck had affixed around his waist, filled with 11 kilograms of Cemtex, the deadliest explosive material that the Soviet era ever produced. The explosion was so powerful, that 60 kilometers away, back at the camp, we vividly felt its tremors, and the mushroom of the bomb was apparent in the early-morning sky.

The explosion had the effect of a 3.7 Richter scale earthquake. The mine, the rebels, Yoram, and the general were all bombed into oblivion. All told, we had achieved a small feat: we had reinstated the monopoly status of NeraGem, decapitated the rebels' leadership, saved the honor of General Food--who immediately gained a martyrdom status--and fed my revenge at Yoram's expense. At the exact same time when the general detonated the device, Selleck and his legionnaires emerged from the bushes around the monastery, and with their able hands slit the throats of the Mossad foot soldiers left behind by Yoram to guard Fatima and the boy. They were immediately brought to safety. When she saw me at the main gate, Fatima ran to me. She was silently crying, with one eye shedding tears of joy for the gained life of her son, and the other mourning the loss of his father.

Two days later, I was back in London. I was to meet with the chairman at the Dorchester. To my surprise, when I arrived at his quarters Nadia Gotryne was there to welcome me. She told me how proud she was of my achievements and how sorry she was about the circumstances that surrounded this mission. I had no answer for her. I was not in a mood for chitchat. I remained cold and distant and patiently waited for the chairman in the living room to get down to business. Sacks, draped in a regal blue suit and a bright tie, appeared in a somewhat somber mood. He greeted me with genuine warmth. He asked me whether I had a nice trip and I thanked him for asking. Sacks did not elaborate on the African matter. He was pleased, it was obvious, and why shouldn't he be? But having sensed some tension in my demeanor, a touch of anger in my voice, and a cruel stare in my eyes, he did not dwell on the past and quickly wanted to talk about my new assignment. At that very moment, and before he could say "Jeeves" or some other name by which he calls his Berber servants, I calmly stood up and to everyone's surprise, I informed my host that my days at Inter-Finance were over. He looked at Nadia as if to find some clues to my behavior. She was in a state of shock, horrified at my insolence, but happily surprised at my courage to turn down the most powerful man in the organization.

"By over you mean, finished?" replied Sacks, while lighting his cigarette.

"I'm afraid it has no other meaning in spoken English, sir," I politely replied.

"And the reason being, my boy?" he continued, talking through his pearly white teeth while still holding the lit cigarette.

"It is because of what you have just said—I am nobody's boy, not anymore."

I then excused myself and without much ado, took off!

MOSES' LEGACY

Soraya met me in Paris. I had arranged for her to travel and re-served a romantic hotel accommodation for the two of us. A perfectly Parisian boutique hotel situated at the Place Des Vosges, one of my favorite spots in the city of lights. We walked, talked and dreamt about a common future. I was getting mushy and suddenly domesticated. Pictures of white linens, satin drapes, lawn mowers, and red tiles were suddenly sifting through my head. I had no specific plans, no serious money, and no idea what to do next with my life. I had made up my mind that my days at Inter-Finance were finally over. I had gained enough experience and built a decent number of business contacts to land me a (normal) job in at a (normal) enterprise. But was it really what I wanted? Normal sounded defeatist to me. A girly whitish color when my fabric was more deer-hunter green. What is normal, anyway? After my short-lived tenure at Inter-Finance, a spy movie would look like a tale of two dull cities. But one glance at Soraya and my mind went back wondering about the advantages of "being Earnest" (just to please Oscar's fans and to make a point with those morons who read my kind of books without having first experienced true English literature).

Soraya was expected to return home after the weekend and I was staying over in Paris to collect my paycheck for my last job. I was also planning to look for one. I had been swimming with the sharks for a long time and at present, fishing for something less hazardous sounded like a good idea. I did not exchange vows, but only serious promises with Soraya. We were to get engaged in the spring and married by Christmas. Yes, me! I was going to announce it to my mom, and Soraya would do the same with her folks. From that magical trip, many things were to stay with me for the rest of my days. The laughter, the joy and the shared hope. We were liberated: me from my illusions and Soraya from her fears.

The next morning, I went to Geneva to collect the dough. Roberto Bussoni was an Italian who worked for a French private bank and had a distinct English look. He wore a tailored gray pinstriped suit, an immaculate white shirt, a classic club tie, silver cuff links, and of all things, brown shoes! Only Italians could wear brown brogues and get away with it. For me it was pure heresy of "savoir vivre" and a serious insult to the classic houses of fashion. A stroll down Saville Row wearing these brogues would undoubtedly provoke a fashionistas' riot. Nothing looked odder or more out of place. It was like Khomeini without a beard--or worse, Mother Theresa in a thong. That was the extent of my surprise every time I looked at Roberto's shoes. On this occasion though, shoes were but a small distraction. I walked into Roberto's office and there I was, face to face with Mark Wiesel, who was the late Rutger Zarmat's chief legal counsel.

Mark stood up, slowly adjusted his blazer jacket, and walked up to me with his hand wide open for a genuine salute. I was shocked, but no less glad to see him. I had not met with any member of

Zarmat's inner circle since his unexpected disappearance--except for Nadia, of course. Mark was the legal ace who had saved Rutger many times from the grips of Lady Justice and from the claws of few other ladies of lesser repute. Mark was very well-respected throughout the organization because of his wisdom and because of his Capitol Hill connections. His father was a fur dealer from Austria who escaped the Nazis, heading to Paris in late 1939, and then moving to New York in the early '40s. Mark went to NYU because Harvard and Yale were still at that time impenetrable WASP bastions and Jews could simply not apply. Mark graduated with top honors, worked at the SEC in Washington, and built an impeccable reputation as a securities lawyer, although he became more of a corporate lobbyist. A lobbyist is of course the American word for legal power brokering at the highest spheres of government--a form of legalized shenanigans.

Wiesel was one top lobbyist who, lately, was doing few odd jobs for Inter-Finance but who kept an intimate rapport with the power circle of the firm. He told me that he was in close contact with Ramsay Sacks since Rutger's accident. Zarmat and Sacks were childhood friends, according to Mark, although I thought Sacks had only mingled with royalty during his tender age, not with haut bourgeois like Zarmat. Ramsay had asked Mark to mediate between us. My departure had been taken rather seriously at Inter-Finance--otherwise why would it be necessary to dispatch Mark Wiesel from NY to patch things up? A check and a thank you note (or not even that) would have sufficed, especially with the way I had stormed out of the Dorchester suite a week ago.

Roberto Bussoni handed me my check, which gave me another shocker. The amount was $500,000, ten times more than what I had expected. It was a bribe more than a mere recognition—a means of putting a down payment on my soul, rather than an end-of-service pay. Frankly, I had no remorse taking the money. I had earned it many times over. I could now walk away, take some time off, and then when fully rested and refreshed find some decent employment. Soraya would be proud of me and happy for my decision. But another look at that check and all of that just faded away. If I could make such money from one job, I could earn millions from more challenging assignments. I could have my own Inter-Finance one day and my Soraya (later?). How could I be so selfish? How could I put my eternal happiness on hold for the sake of short-term material success? How could I, how how, but I finally did! (I bet I did not surprise some of you folks who do not think of me as a decent, tax-paying, God-fearing, and one-woman-loving individual. You had it for me from the beginning of this book. For all of you who thought that way, you have been vindicated. You have been wise. For all of you who have thought otherwise, you have been had for your money. But be content, since it is just a paperback at an affordable price.)

Mark invited me to lunch at the Hotel du Rhones. The hotel was packed as usual and the dining room was filled with Geneva's Who's Who. You can only catch a glimpse of them at lunchtime since the official bedtime in Geneva is 7:00 p.m. The only people who ventured out at night or stayed awake during the early hours of the morning were the Russian hookers and the Turkish janitors, each getting screwed by the Swiss, but in a different way. That you could count on. That was Swiss exactitude. The Swiss trains and all the rest. Mark did not waste any more time, and asked what would it take to bring me back to Inter-Finance. My reply was simple: more power, and much more money. I wanted both recognition and position. I would no longer act as a gofer for the top brass. I knew too much, and had kept my mouth shut.

I delivered without fuss or fanfare. That Mark clearly understood and Ramsay appreciated. The good thing about clever people like Mark is that human behavior scarcely surprises them. Mark opened his brief case and handed me a "Blue Contract Form": the partnership bond! The ultimate business aphrodisiac light years before the blue pill itself. Nothing could have made me happier. I took it in my hands. I turned its mere two pages, looked at the seven-figure amount, sneaked a peek at the profit-sharing percentage, glanced at the dotted line with a serial number next to it that indicated the limited edition, and smiled. Mark, proud like a father on a graduation day, offered me his fountain pen and I obliged. Voilà! Finally a Brahmin. Outcast no more. Officially a member of the inner circle of this corporate fraternity whose reign and supremacy now became part of my own destiny.

The plan was made simple. Mark and I would meet Ramsay Sacks in Paris during the weekend to talk about my new assignment. Sacks was staying at the Plaza Athene. In the meantime, Mark asked me to meet a Canadian fellow who managed one of Inter-Finance's largest mining and minerals companies. I wasn't given the reason for the meeting. The venue was set at Inter-Finance's offices in Geneva. The next morning, Jason Conrad was expecting me, wearing plaid khaki pants and a navy-blue blazer. He looked just like a prep school boy who overgrew his uniform and lost the pimples on the way, but kept the smirk. The man was tall, clean-cut and looked straight like all Canadians do--the North American version of the Swiss, and with a French patois to boot. "*Oui Monsieur, Vive le Quebec Libre!*" Jason punctuated his monologue with short sentences and long pauses.

The affiliate of Inter-Finance, he was in charge of "Philadelphia Minerals," one of the world's largest producers of potash. Of what, I ventured? In plain English, it was a natural fertilizer used primarily in agriculture. It is extracted from mines or other natural locations in the form of salt and then processed in granular forms, bagged, and sold like any other commodity. I must confess that prior to this revelation I had no idea that potash existed or that it was used to grow tomatoes. Great, now we know all this and would alert the Discovery Channel! Quite a big promotion for an assignment, I thought. From diamonds, the most pure and elegant form of natural resources worn by hot chicks, to natural salt that is spread over fried chicks. Except that Conrad, smarting from my apparent lack of interest in his stuff, went on to explain that Philadelphia Minerals extracted its potash from the Dead Sea--on the Jordanian side, that is. Because there are two sides to Conrad's story...and to the Dead Sea, too. The Dead Sea, for those of you who need a mental compass to follow and which for your luck I have been carrying all over this novel, is situated between today's Jordan (yesterday's Trans-Jordan) and today's Israel (yesterday's Palestine). The sea salt is easily scooped from the brims of the Dead Sea and processed in giant pans till it becomes potash--one of the most economical extraction processes in the world. Nature has helped, making it easy for these guys. It was Moses' legacy. Potash producers globally went through very sophisticated excavating methods to dig up this natural resource from deep mines in Canada and the Ural Mountains.

Enough with Mining & Minerals 101. What was the problem, I asked? Well, you see, Jason said, production was sold in Europe, Asia, and the Near East. Prices were determined by many factors, including world economic growth, agricultural production, climate, and transportation costs. But Philadelphia Minerals was a natural giant. It recorded significant margins due to the inexpensive upstream process. Another competitive advantage was its proximity to consuming markets, especially Southeast Asia and the Near East. The end products were sold through a network of global dealers acting as brokers between producers (such as Philadelphia Minerals), and large consumers (such as farming co-ops in India). Philadelphia Minerals set prices worldwide as the world's swing producer, just like Saudi in OPEC. But here came the catch. In the past twelve months, the largest wholesale traders in Europe and Asia seemed to have (literally) vanished and were taken over by a virtual cartel which started—in a reverse course--to dictate prices upon Philadelphia Minerals. This newly formed cartel of dealers appeared to control all the value chain from purchasing to transportation. This left Philadelphia Minerals at their mercy with the residual, low-margin task of extraction. Thus, one of the cash cows of Inter-Finance (yearly net income of circa $250 million) was turning into a donkey.

Inter-Finance had secured, through the impeccable connections of Rutger Zarmat with the royals in Jordan, a 110-year production sharing agreement, which required the annual payment of royalties levied on every ton of potash lifted on cargo from the Port of Aqaba.

I left Geneva in a hurry, with a story that was taking a strange turn. There was a group of vanishing potash dealers, an emerging mystery cartel that was cornering the market, and, as a result, an Inter-Finance subsidiary bleeding losses in our hands. (You noticed the "our" hands?! I was part owner now.) Nothing made any sense. Potash, no disrespect to Jason, was neither oil nor silver nor diamonds for a change. This was potash, for God's sake! Who would want to "corner" the potash market? It surely was not a headline-grabbing story. No major wire service, journal, or

half-assed reporter had written about it. No op-eds by left lean-
ing economists denouncing this situation and defending the right
of every meek and wretched farmer of the world to grow their
veggies at subsidized prices! While this saga was ongoing, the
world seemed oblivious to it.

I joined Ramsay and Mark in the "Bar Anglais" at the Plaza
Athene, just where Rutger Zarmat used to invite me for a chat
when we happened to be in Paris. It was a discreet, dimly lit, and
very warm place, especially at lunchtime, when no one else was
around except the Brazilian bartender who knew your favorite
drink before you even ordered it. My kind of dive. The trip to
Paris by train provided me with the opportunity to rethink this
matter. We had to find out what had happened to the main potash dealers who were previously operating out of Europe. Their
fate was intimately related to the rest of the story. They held the
key to this enigma. Jason Conrad insisted that they had vanished,
just like that. How could this be possible? I probed him time
and time again. Did they close shop, relocate, sell out? He knew
nothing. Sacks had—as usual--some useful leads on this front. He
gave me the name of one of the largest trading firms of potash
products: the mighty Continental Traders, domiciled in Brussels.
Continental Traders moved markets and influenced prices
through close ties with shipping lines in Holland and Greece.

The owner was a fellow who went by the (Belgian) name of
Jacques Brezwigt. It sounded Belgian, all right, just like Waterloo
or Zebruge! He had reportedly sold his company in a private
transaction few months ago. All we knew was that the new owners kept the trading operations intact but renamed the company
"Eastern Seaports." The company's trading empire span into Asia
where it controlled large networks of sub-dealers operating out

of Singapore. Sacks, as usual, was five steps ahead of us all. He had investigated the whereabouts of Brezwigt and had sighted him in Rome. The problem, though, was that no one had ever seen Brezwuigt in person or knew what he looked like. Rome was a very large city in which to find a faceless Belgian. Sacks gave me the name of our Italian contact, "a trusted man," in his own words: Signor Armando Domani. I was expected to call him upon my arrival in Rome, tonight. Sacks did not mention the Blue Contract. I bid my host farewell, and started my Roman journey.

When I finally arrived by train, Rome was rather empty at this late hour of the night. The Excelsior was a splendid hotel with all the accoutrements of a true Italian palazzo that had survived the modern age without losing its Renaissance spirit. I walked into my junior suite and was in awe at the sight of the high ceilings, the antique furniture, and the regal office corner. It was an ideal place for a romantic escapade, not for a manhunt. Let us recapitulate. Philadelphia Minerals was literally on the verge of financial collapse, and could not control potash prices, let alone selling its products to anyone except the new mystery cartel. How and why did potash elicit so much attention? Brezwigt must have had the inside track, since he skipped the arena and got away with the dough while he could. To whom had he sold his company? What were the motives of the buyers? Into my briefcase, Jason Conrad had slipped a detailed study on the chemical components of potash--not an exciting subject. Potash was basically the salt of the earth--or of the Dead Sea, more appropriately. Ironically, it did well for the earth in terms of fertilizing crops, but not for the sea. No living marine life (wild or mild) could ever survive the salty levels of the Dead Sea...no fishing potential to speak of. Although human sharks were in abundance on both sides of the Jordan River, none could venture into its salty waters, as if Moses wanted to leave us a legacy cloaked in an unsolvable riddle. A sea, which is supposed to nurture living things, was pronounced clinically dead because of the very salt it contained and which is used to make all living things grow. Enough with cheap Kabala interpretations and into the cabaret, I figured.

I was dead set on visiting the Jacky O, the infamous nightclub of my famous hotel. I descended into the dungeon without anticipation. At the club's door stood two bouncers who looked like Roman gladiators, but in Armani suits. Their shirt buttons were about to burst at any slight move of the torso. I showed them my room key and their pit bull grins changed into sissy smiles. Why do I always detect some effeminate attitude in the most macho-looking men? Why is it that the more muscles you put on, the tougher you look, and the softer you end up being? Conversely, I have seen the most ferocious attitudes from gays. At least, I was sure about my orientation and was looking for a similarly inclined, consenting, (opposite sex) adult.

The Jacky O was full. The dancing floor was packed with no signs of retrieve from the happy goers who were swinging to the tunes of Black Box, my favorite pop group of the '80s. (Please refrain from your opinionated comments on this subject in particular. I take dancing music very seriously, Black Box being the Uber Jungle Chant). So while I was gently moving with the rhythms, I spotted a red-haired mermaid on the other side of the floor. She was sitting at a crowded table, with other young friends who were chatting loudly--judging from their lips--most probably because of the blasting music. The mermaid sat quietly, somewhat distancing herself from the group, while displaying distinct signs of boredom, looking intermittently at her nails (strike one), at her wristwatch (strike two), and at the ceiling (strike three!). I swiftly cut through the dance floor, and dodged some serious butt kicks thrown by enthused dancers who were really trying hard to imitate Travolta, with his same greasy and vulgar style. I landed on the other side apparently unharmed. I walked up to her and asked the time. She was surprised but answered with wit and a devastating smile, "It is way past the bedtime of little boys." I quickly replied that my parents were abducted by pirates, my baby sitter had run out with Peter Pan, and the only way to find my way back to my room was to be escorted by Tinkerbell. How about that for a little boy story? I made her smile and won a spot on the edge of her seat.

Her name was Wendy. She was from San Fran, visiting Rome with a bunch of girlfriends on a European tour. They were all staying at the Albergo Della Città some sort of a local Ramada Inn (no offense to the salesmen on the road.) We both agreed that the music was too loud to be able to have any decent conversation and decided to take a walk on the calm side.

Once out of the disco I took a closer look at Wendy. She was tall, it and well-fitted in her tight black dress. An all-American beauty, whatever that may mean to you. To me it means all beautiful Yankee gals, excluding the Hamptons summer crowd, California bimbos on Rodeo Drive, Bostonian brahmins on Beacon Hill, and lesbians anywhere (*no matter how pretty they look*). Wendy was a true slice of apple pie. (Yes, another cliché just to remind you of the pathetic narration of this book and push you harder to leave it on the kitchen table, or in the toilet. In any event, it may be a good idea now to start thinking of doing something more useful with your lives. Getting one, that is!) She caught me gazing at her and was amused by my stare. She proposed we visit a cozy café on Piazza Di Spagna where we could get hot drinks and get further acquainted—orally, that is.

Wendy, as the story went, was a marine biologist. She worked in the Bay Area with the World Marine Fund. (Your basic dolphin lover, or tuna-fishing hater, for the idiot green activists who happen to be reading this book.) There I was, sitting next to Flipper's best friend. Once she started talking about her work, nothing could stop her diatribe, and the lecture alternated between imminent sea pollution, shortage of plankton, disappearing underwater creatures, and your usual effluents and currents. I must have looked convincingly interested (and awake, thanks to the double espressos the waiter kept pouring), 'cause Wendy gave me a full-sized discourse fit for print in Cousteau's Underwater Encyclopedia. Frankly, my exposure to "water world" was strictly limited to my daily shower. Water was not my cup of tea (or of sea? bad joke, I concede, now back to Deep Blue). After touring the oceans, Wendy got finally curious about my job, so I spilled my classic "international consultant" tale. She swallowed it. No joke!

Her friends had convinced her to take a summer tour of Europe and the first leg of their trip happened to be Rome. They stayed at a budget hotel but lived above their budgets, judging from their clubbing habits and Wendy's Walter Steiger shoes. The Jacky O was not for mere plebeians in Rome. Rome itself was not an easy venue, so what were these California girls doing here, and how would they know about the in-places in town? Wendy offered an explanation. One of her friends was dating an Italian count (with a big bank account, I presumed) who lived in Rome and worked as a curator at the Vatican Museum. That's how she got the inside track on what's hot and what's not in Roma. It happened that the same count was organizing a party at his palazzo in Rome the next day. Wendy asked if I would like to come. A girl was asking me out in the nicest way possible. Not being used to this kind of friendly gestures from the female gender, I hesitated to respond. I did not know what to say, and finally uttered something about not being sure that I could make it, but that I would do my best. Undeterred by my lame reply, Wendy scribbled on the tablecloth the address of the count's mansion and said that she would be pleased if I could make it.

Time was getting late—way past little boys' and little girls' bedtime--and we decided to part company. We left the café, and hailed a cab despite the late hour. I escorted Wendy to the car's back door, and as if synchronized by an opera conductor, we both swirled in each other's direction and kissed for a long moment. It was long enough for the cabby to become frustrated with our love scene and to impatiently ask where we were heading. Without hesitation and with a renewed cockiness, I shouted "Excelsior!" The short ride to my hotel was simply magic. Wendy's lips tasted like burning caramel. We kissed without a word, or a moan, or any of those public displays of affection that newfound lovers are so fond of showing. When we arrived in my suite, we embraced and innocently spooned on the sofa.

When I woke up the next day it was past 10:00 a.m. I was alone in bed and Wendy had obviously left without a sound. The phone was flashing intermittently, signaling a voice message. I guessed right--it was Armando Domani, the ace contact of Inter-Finance. He had been waiting for me in the hotel lobby since 8:30 a.m. I jumped from the bed in a flash, showered, got dressed, and ran down the swirling marble staircase. Armando was sitting in the lobby, and looked as he had drunk the hotel's entire cappuccino stock and read all the morning papers while waiting for my unceremonious arrival. With a brisk walk, to make up for lost time, I crossed the lobby going in his direction and asked for his forgiveness, in a genuine tone. Armando was princely about my lack of punctuality.

Since I did not dare offer him anything (more) to drink, I went straight to the point. We needed to find the Belgian trader, I said. He had been recently spotted in Rome. With all the money that he must have pocketed from the sale of Continental Traders, I frankly could not think of a better place to select for permanent domicile. The scenery is second to none (just compare it with foggy London), the food is delicious (keep on comparing with English cuisine) and the wine was as good as the French (but at half price). Granted, a Belgian could not live on such refinements alone, but I figured that French fries and poor-quality beer were also available in Italy, right? Armando needed some clues to start his search. As we lacked such leads, Armando decided to start with the contacts he had with the local police, the famous Italian Carabinieri…the only police force in the world whose job was not to protect and serve the people, but the Cosa Nostra. (No, it is not a restaurant! it is Italian for the mob). All in the family, from the smallest trattoria to the largest industrial conglomerate in Italy, all were connected to the mob. So why go to the police, I asked? Let us go directly to the mob, I suggested.

At that moment, Armando took his time (just as I did before, at his expense) and explained how things worked in modern Italy. Same as in ancient Italy, mind you but worthy of listening to. First you contact a "wired bird" (a high-ranking police officer with irreproachable links to the mob). This "wired bird" takes you to a "mule" (a connected person who would only carry your message). If the deal were of any interest to the Cosa Nostra (not a restaurant again), the "mule" would fix a meeting where you would meet a "made man" (a senior member of the family, or the crew--not from an airline, mind you). The "made man" would submit a proposal in exchange for the favor you were about to ask of him. If you could deliver on the proposal and show proof, then the "made man" would finally take you for a parley with a "capo" (the boss). Terms would be agreed and favors exchanged. That's how it worked. All the roads led to Rome but it was only the shortcuts that allowed you to arrive safely. Any slippage on the way and you might end up missing until recovered from a river bed, with both feet planted in freshly mixed cement. Enough with the macabre descriptions. Armando had arranged a chat with a "wired bird," Colonel Dutti.

"Generalissimo Dutti, we desperately need your help," said Armando to the obviously pleased officer. His promotion to general did not fall on deaf ears. The colonel's face beamed like a billboard "Generalissimo," Armando insisted, "we are on the lookout for someone who happens to be in Rome. He has been eluding us for a while. Getting to him is a matter of grave importance to Inter-Finance and to your finances, if you catch my drift?"

Dutti was still beaming from the flattery and did not realize that we were waiting for an answer. After an uncomfortable pause of some considerable minutes, "Si, si si," he furtively replied. "I understand tutto, OK, OK?"

Armando, ever the smooth operator, had brought with him a Bible that was previously emptied of its godly scriptures and filled with $100 bills of In God We Trust. Dutti took the Bible, opened it, and had an epiphany. "I want a meeting with a made man today," I said.

"No, no, no," Dutti replied, "this is too soon, too soon."

It could not be arranged, he insisted. I looked at Armando, who then pulled a concise but still bulky version of an encyclopedia from his briefcase. That was loaded with $1000 bills. Dutti almost fell from his chair. He just could not cope with $250K sitting on his office desk--'cause mind you, we were still at the HQ of the Roman police. Come to think of it, no other place would have been safer to carry this kind of cash around. Dutti's face returned to its beaming mode with a turbo charge this time. He scribbled an address on a piece of paper, handed it to me and said to Armando in Italian, as was later translated, to be at the rendezvous no later than 6:00 p.m. We shook hands, and took off.

Armando drove me back to the hotel so we could check on our messages. Nothing. Sacks must have been very busy, I figured, otherwise he would have been all over me with probing questions. I was too tired to carry on an intelligent conversation, and decided to take a nap. Armando was going to pick me up from the Excelsior shortly before the meeting. Our destination was a racetrack located some forty-five minutes outside the city center. As our meeting was scheduled for 6:00 p.m,, Armando suggested that he return by 5:00 p.m. and drive me to our blind date. I thought of Wendy's invitation and figured that after the encounter at the tracks I might still be able to make it to the party. With that lovely thought, I hit the sack, only to wake up few minutes before our agreed departure time. I hurriedly changed my clothes, and met Armando by the front entrance of the hotel. We drove fast, and did not talk much on the way. I sensed that Armando was a bit nervous--or afraid, maybe? He was not the type of man who dealt with criminals. He was a refined, Italian middleman with manners and mannerisms. He had been accustomed to securing contacts for Inter-Finance acting as the senior advisor to both Zarmat and Sacks for matters such as oil deals with Libya. He felt uneasy on this assignment. I could sense it. We arrived at the main gate, a bit ahead of schedule. We parked the car and went straight to the Ambassadors' Lounge, as scribbled in Dutti's note.

When we entered, the odor of Cuban cigars filled the room, mixed with strong Guerlain perfume, champagne, and the distinctive smell of money being laid on the tracks. The hostess who greeted us introduced herself and gently directed us toward a short man with a welcoming smile. In broken English "Jaccomo Obletti" welcomed us with open arms, literally. He was dressed like a well-to-do merchant on a Sunday afternoon: shiny white shoes and pearly teeth. Mr. Obletti showed us to our seats and invited us to watch the thirtd race of the day. A bay horse, The Avalon was the race's favorite. From the start the jockeys were engaged in a frenzied competition. The horses were stretched, covering the tracks with increasingly wider strides. The crowd was cheering with enthusiasm rarely seen in (civilized) horse races. The Avalon was leading by a wide margin, unconcerned by the rest of the equine creatures behind it, distant and almost serene, very secure in his animal power.

On that last turn and before the final stretch to the finishing line, a stick battle erupted between the jockeys of the two mounts just behind The Avalon, throwing it farther ahead, and when all bets were off, and The Avalon assured of the trophy, it suddenly collapsed, a few meters before the flag post, leaving No. 7, Charm Bracelet, to take home an undeserved victory. The scene was apocalyptic. The Avalon was flat on its back, as if ravaged by violent spasms. The jockey was not moving, lying down a few meters away, most probably with a fatal injury. The horse was in excruciating pain, experiencing a slow but sure death. It was a tragic moment for the fans and a great disappointment, no doubt, for the owners. Obletti was calmly following the unfolding events with his golden binoculars. I thought I detected a smile on his face. He looked unsurprised by the results of the race. Something in my guts told me that Obletti was not a made man but more probably a capo.

Obletti sat down on the huge leather sofa and turned to me. He plainly asked how he could be of assistance. I gave him the long and short about Continental Traders while he listened carefully to my description of the missing Brezwigt. He immediately grasped the critical importance of this matter to Inter-Finance and its principals. Looking me straight in the eyes, with his hands crossed, Obletti told me that he could find our man, dead or alive, in a matter of forty-eight hours, only if I could return the favor. Obletti, I realized was the ultimate padrino. (Did you know that padrino comes not from some Mario Puzo mob movie but from paterfamilias, the ancient Roman system of fatherly power? Sure you did--silly me; I have a real cultured bunch reading my book. Keep on forgetting). Bravo Dutti! The miracle of the Bible did pay off. Then came my question about the favor. Obletti went on saying that Inter-Finance had some of the best contacts in the Arabian Gulf, which was home of first-class breeders. These horse lovers regularly participated in all landmark races from Hong Kong to Saratoga and from Ascot to Deauville. One particular family from the Emirates, the Mabrouks, was dominant in this business. Listening to him, I naively thought that he wanted to buy a purebred Arabian from the Mabrouks--a Darley

Arabian, so to speak, that would come from Arabia Felix to Old Europe and cover mares with semen and its owners with glory.

Sensing my confusion, Obletti said in a calm voice, "Those Mabrouks are no ordinary Bedouins. They have the money and the vision to do great things. A very rare combination nowadays," he insisted, and I concurred, nodding my head nervously. "They want to build an Arabian-styled Las Vegas to become the ultimate stop-over for all frustrated Arabs, embargoed Persians, deprived Near Easterners and lowlife Brits looking for nighttime fun, daytime sun, and money on the run." (So it rhymes! What's your problem? You were expecting Shakespeare?)

This kind of city could become a lightning rod for the world's most vicious drug dealers, professional gamblers and con artists, prostitutes, pimps, and serial killers looking for a new frontier. To run such city would require discipline and order, of the sort that no police force in the world–let alone in the Third World--can provide. Only the Cosa Nostra could be of assistance to ring-fence this city and contain the spillover effects of criminality that accompany the rise of every metropolis. *Where is the favor?* I kept asking myself? The answer was close. The Mabrouks had to agree on fixing three out of seven world races of their own choosing, and in exchange, the Cosa Nostra would protect their city.

We took leave from the boss (padrino in English, you fools!) and went back to Rome. Armando was jubilant, having succeeded in his mission. What would be the reaction of Sacks? Was dealing with the mob, and asking embarrassing favors from ruling families in the Gulf worth this Brezwigt?

I decided to go to Wendy's palazzo party after all, but first, I had to make a detailed report to Sacks. I called him on a secured line. He was satisfied with the quick results and did not comment on the nature of the favor. The night was young and I followed my heart while the Italian cab driver followed his instincts to find the palazzo. Cracking the potash puzzle was hard but not impossible. The cab fare—on the other hand--was both hard and impossible. The palazzo looked old, as it should be, and well-lit, with a large garden flowing from the entrance gate to the back of the mansion. My name was on the guest list, curiously enough, and I was pleased that the spelling was correct. It really matters to me how one writes, reads, and pronounces my name. Wendy had passed this test with ease.

Guests were mingling in the ballroom. Wendy saw me and waved from afar. She came almost running, smiling and obviously happy to see me. "You made it after all," she murmured. I just smiled and gave her a kiss on the cheek. She wanted to introduce me to our host, Count Silvio Rizzi, a curator of art at the Vatican Museum--a tall, grey-haired gentleman who spoke perfect English, for a change. We exchanged pleasantries and talked about Roman art, which lies in tons in the Levant: the Empire's first law schools, public baths, temples, castles, hippodromes, stadiums, and aqueducts. My knowledge of archeology was nil, but you did not need to be an expert to acknowledge the beauty and charms of the ancient world compared to the ugliness of the new one, including the Eiffel Tower, the Sears Tower..and yes, Tower Records!

Suddenly, Wendy got all agitated when a small, balding, and self-effacing gentleman entered the room. Count Silvio asked her—as if to prevent a brawl--to remain calm and to keep her distance from this guest. I politely inquired about the gentleman and the Count, ever a diplomat, told me in a whisper voice that he was the

Chairman of Azzurra, the largest five-star hotel and resort chain in the world. That did not help me one bit. He hurried the explanation. Azzurra was developing four sites in the Mediterranean and one in the Caribbean. This last one seriously threatened all marine life from dolphins to the coral reef habitat. Wendy was a staunch ecosystem activist for marine causes–as I already knew--and had traded some blows in public with this gentleman at the World EcoSystem Forum, last winter. The evening was going to be fun, I guessed. I turned to Wendy, whose face was getting red and puffed up by the minute, and asked her to dance. She obliged, but not without a moment of hesitation. While dancing I told her how admiring I was of her noble fight to save mammals and plankton. She was obviously pleased. I really thought that the more good people (like Wendy) got busy in non-profit matters, the more profits would be left to shysters (like me).

A gentle bell ring summoned the guests to dinner. The table was simply magnificent, and each had a designated seat. The Azzura chairman sat across from me while his wife sat to my right. Wendy was purposely seated at a good distance from him, but that did not stop her from exchanging her seat with another guest and landing a chair right next to Mr. Rizzi. This being a civilized dinner, I hoped no major disturbances would take place. Wendy was apparently nervous, while Mr. Rizzi was getting tensed up. His wife, conversely, was relaxed--almost too relaxed, judging from her wandering hand that set on a lone search for my lower body parts. I smiled, looked at her, and discreetly pushed back her not-so-subtle incursion. She smiled but did not budge one inch, oblivious to my resistance, just like Napoleon at Waterloo facing a stiff Wellington and hordes of Prussian troops who backed him. (For a historical intermission, allow me to press the case that it was the good old Germans--not the Brits--who won that battle under Von Blucher, whereby a Corsican--not a Frenchman--lost, but the Brits still claimed victory. Same as in World War II... Britain started the fight, but someone else finished it.) I figured if Wendy wanted to socially harass the husband, it was only fair to allow the wife to sexually harass me! (See how egalitarian I am?)

Surprisingly, Wendy stayed calm while the antipasto was served, but by the time of the main course she started raising her voice a few decibels more, and began hurling insults at the resort developer, who remained fairly calm. But the same could not be said of his wife. She was now using all the might of her left arm to overtake my upper right thigh and I had to physically restrain her from hurting my gentler parts. Maybe while her husband was busy building new resorts, I was her last! The exchange between Wendy and her nemesis became so embarrassing that it was time to take charge of the situation. I stood up—to the obvious chagrin of the wife--and asked Wendy—to the apparent delight of the husband--to accompany me to the garden for some fresh air. Wendy obliged grudgingly and raced me to the front gate. She apologized for having behaved so badly and I tried to belittle the distracting moment of our evening by focusing on the more exciting moments yet to come.

By now, few guests were left and fine liquor and cigars were on offer in the inner courtyard of the palazzo. Our host was a highly educated person who discussed only topics he mastered well. We were treated to a lecture on the obsessions of the Medicis about power and art, the pathological nature of the Borgias, the megalomaniac streak of Mussolini, and the intrigues of the Black Pope (the nickname given to the highest priest in the Jesuit order. Free education for the masses is a form of charity, I reckon). Most guests looked interested; I looked the part, while getting sleepy. Shortly thereafter, Wendy left the party and headed back to the Excelsior. Once in the lobby, and before I could hope for a charming (live) dessert, Armando Domani was waiting for me by the elevator as if visited by a ghost. He gestured frantically and I quickened my steps toward him to have a private word before Wendy could catch up with us.

"They got him," he said, and before I was able to react, he pushed me into a corner and in the same depressed voice said, "they got the Belgian trader." I was mum. I snapped into action and told Wendy to wait for me in the suite, while I had to deal with some urgent business (at 1:00 a.m., that must be a first). She was too tired to argue and, obliged gracefully.

We hopped into Armando's car and drive to the address given by Dutti, the top honcho policeman. Fast-forward twenty minutes, and I was in the emergency hall of Rome's Central Hospital. Dutti was already at the scene, waiting for us with his hands in his raincoat and his eyes gazing at the sky. (Picture *Casablanca,* the corrupt high-ranking French police officer; is there any other kind?). Dutti looked at me with empty eyes and said in his broken English (he never realized that he could utter few words of distinct Shakespearian quality, but he tried, right?) that they found the Belgian trader in a posh villa on the outskirts of Rome. He had overdosed on heroin (not French fries?!). He was in that morbid state for few hours before the police arrived at the scene, tipped by no less than their best informants (read: the mob). *How efficient,* I thought, *but how useless.* Now we were indebted to Obletti and committed to carry out the Mabrouks' deal, all in exchange for a dead corpse. We asked the mob for a hot tip, but we got a cold stiff instead! We never specified whether we wanted the runaway trader: dead or alive! We never thought we needed to. Now we had to honor our end of the bargain. We lost and they won. And guess whose head Sacks was going to chew off?!

I insisted on going to the morgue. I had never seen the gentleman alive and now I had the curiosity of seeing him devoid of life. The blanket was lifted and the sight was there for all of us to savor: a huge inert mass of white fat and blond hair. He could not tell us anything and we could not gather a clue from him-- not in this state, I mean. I turned to Armando and gave him a direct order not to inform Sacks, as of yet. The newspapers too needed to be muzzled for forty-wight hours. Sacks read *Corriere della Sera* every day to check the Italian borsa and the latest political gossip. I bet he read the obituaries too. Armando, I insisted, had to use his connections with the media to stop the story from finding its way to the printing press. We had nothing in hand, and Sacks might rethink the Mabrouks' deal while we were still in need of the mob, and while I was still physically in Italy. (Do you get the drift, or have you put down this book for tonight? Too much excitement or too much complication for your little cerebral box, heh?) I did not want to end up like the potash peddler. I still had some gas in my tank and wanted to go all the way, but not this way! Armando, shocked at the sight of the dead man, did not have the stomach to question my judgment or debate my orders. Judging from his appearance, Armando was about to faint, or vomit, or opt for an early retirement...all being poor choices at present. Tonight I needed everyone sharp, ready, and capable of functioning albeit at a lower mental voltage than usual.

We all agreed to meet at Dutti's office the next morning at noon. I asked him if he could send me back to the hotel in one of his police cars so I could speed up my return to finish the evening with Wendy. He obliged and I got in one of the Alfa Romeos that had been recalibrated to suit the driving habits of the carabinieris of Roma. For sure, I was treated to an insane (but enjoyable) drive, with loud sirens, flashing lights, and no chance of getting a speeding ticket! That is what I called a free ride.

Back at the hotel, Wendy was all gone. She had left me a scribbled message near the bed table. She wrote it in code-like language. "Had to Go. Terrible Tragedy in the Sultanate of Oman. Will Call Later." That was it. A vanished trader and a vanished date. *Too much for one evening*, I thought. Wendy gave up on me, after my last-minute dash to attend to some business emergency. Maybe it was for the best. I needed to collect my thoughts, not my trophies. Would the secret of the potash be lost forever with the death of our Belgian friend, or could I probe the mob for more clues about the villa, the source of the heroin, and the places that our man frequented while in Rome? All these were questions worth asking. Would the mobsters give us a clue before we delivered on the equine deal? I doubted it, but I also needed to stall them. I had to gain some ground before being buried under it. My best choice at this instant was a glass of cognac and some sleep. I went with this brilliant plan with my eyes wide shut.

The first thing I did in the morning was to call Wendy. She was sobbing. She was hysterical, to be more precise. Apparently, an eco-disaster had occurred off the coast of Oman, at the Island of Masirah. The island was 95 km long north-south, between 12 and 14 km wide, with an area of about 649 km², and a population estimated at 12,000 in 12 villages mainly in the north of the island. The principal village was Ras-Hilf in the northern part of the island. It contained a Royal Air Force of Oman air base and a fish factory, as well as a few small towns. Apart from the geography lesson of Oman, it was there that a whole colony of endangered sea turtles was virtually wiped out. From endangered to gone, overnight. "Was it the flu?" I asked. (But they were sea turtles; how would they catch the flu?!) My sense of (bad) morning humor was lost on Wendy.

"How could you laugh at such a matter?" she replied.

Now my endangered relation with Wendy was going from rocky to bottom! "Did they know the reason?" I asked, and she said with a terse tone that the salt level in the ocean went up unexpectedly to norms never monitored before. The turtles' biological system could not cope with it and they had died from what she called an overdose of salt! When she said the words overdose and salt in the same sentence, a giant lamp lit in my brain. I finished the conversation with Wendy better than I started it, and promised to see her and console her in the afternoon.

I immediately got on the phone and called Selleck, my mercenary friend. He was in South Africa, of all places. "Shooting some elephants?" I asked.

"No just some bad asses," he casually replied. "Can't even sell their carcasses for any value."

I told him that I needed a favor and he obliged. I was intrigued about Oman and the Masirah Island, and asked whether he had any clues about it? He started laughing and asked me if I was getting into the spying game? "No," I replied, "what's the skinny on that one?"

Well, the Island of Masirah as it turned out, was leased for fifty years from the Sultan of Oman by the US Navy as a relay naval base to Diego Garcia, the other key naval base used by the Yanks for operations in the Indian Ocean and the Persian Gulf. It is off-limits to intruders, except for the native fishermen and the turtles who have adopted the island as a perfect home for laying and hatching their eggs. (Well, I hope you like them sunny side up with a pinch of salt, I said to my wicked mind. I couldn't help it, so buzz off.) Selleck had friends on the island, a certain Lt. Colonel Kevin Chassengill who could give me more info if I needed. I asked him if he could get me on the damn island and he just burst into another streak of laughter. No! That was just impossible, but Sacks could, he added. That hurt.

I let him go back to his hunting party and dialed Sacks' private number at the Dorchester without hesitation. It was 10:00 a.m. London time and he picked up the call. Usually, he did not take calls before noon. I came out clean and told him the night's ordeal, the discovery of the overdosed trader. He took it rather well, except when I brought up the subject of Oman. "What does Oman have to do with it?" he asked? I told him that there was a link, I was sure, and that I could prove it if only I could visit the island for few hours. He was not convinced and dismissed my theories. I had no theories on this one, I said, but a damned good hunch. He berated me further, and said he would come back to me in a while, after making few calls to fix the Mabrouks' deal. He agreed to honor our debt to the mob, because that was his style: honor and duty above all. He disagreed with me on everything else. But I was not about to give up.

I called Armando and we both went to see Wendy. Once at her place, I asked her about finding a way of getting me into the island disguised as a Greenpeace activist! I wanted to help and my business connections would greatly advance her cause, I assured her. She was elated, thinking that I had turned Green (or is it pink?). I explained the security situation on the island and she acknowledged the difficulties, but under the circumstances, she was sure that the US Navy would not oppose peaceful ecological experts from entering the zone to assess the real damage and take Samples from dead turtles. To make her happy, I promised to put pressure on the Azzura chairman (of the kind that his wife had put on me, and in the same exact spot) to redesign his newly announced resort in Barbados in an environmentally friendly fashion. That sealed the deal. A few hours later, I had all the genuinely false credentials of a first-class tree-hugging environmentalist on his way to assess the disastrous consequences of the carnage that had befallen the Omani turtles. Our plane was leaving at 5:00 p.m. and two additional "real" experts were accompanying me on this field trip.

The flight was bumpy but safe. The landing was smooth, but the reception was not. The plane was immediately surrounded on arrival by five Jeeps of US Military Police, shouting at the top of their lungs with indiscernible orders. We disembarked and were escorted each separately in a Jeep flanked by some muscular Marines. Our papers were checked and we were taken by helicopter to the site. No pictures were allowed, no radio transmitting devices, no nothing. We observed the horrific scenery with bewilderment: thousands of turtles, floating in the sea, while a few others had drifted to the shore, dead still. Not a pretty sight by any stretch of the imagination, whether you were a friend of Bambi or of Rambo. The sheer image of death in such gigantic proportions caused me pain and anger. The dead turtles were floating on the surface as if weightless. "It's the damn salt level!" said one of our minders. "It will take some time to wash off with the rising tide," he added.

We brought our test tubes, took samples and bagged afew dead turtles to be studied by the vet labs, back in Rome. On our way back to the base, I inquired about the whereabouts of Lt. Colonel Chassengill. That question earned me some respect from our detail that asked me to ride in the front, leaving the other (real) experts in the back. Selleck's connections would help me again. From the Jeep, I was put in contact with this Chassengill fellow, who did not have the faintest idea who I was. When I mentioned Georges Selleck his voice became friendlier and he promised to meet me at our arrival point.

Chassengill was not your typical Marine officer. Picture one mean hard-ass soldier and multiply that by five and you get closer to the mountain of bricks I was standing next to. After the welcoming handshake (it was more like a hand mowing), he asked me how I knew Selleck and I gave him some story of a related female cousin who worked for the Peace Corps and who had introduced us a while ago. How else could I connect the macho Selleck with a Greenpeace activist?! He laughed and told me that he had met Selleck many years ago when the US Marines had joint trainings with the French Foreign Legion, with whom Selleck served at the time. They both went AWOL from the Legion's base in Corsica for absence of active duty (read: no ongoing war) in Africa that summer. The training was too dull for their taste, so they jumped ship and went fighting with the Taliban in the Khaibar Pass, in the middle of Pashtun land. Can you believe these guys?

Chassengill was military intel. He knew all that was worth noticing in his perimeter. I ventured a question about his take on the turtle disaster and he gave me what sounded at first a far-fetched answer. His version of the events had its source in the reports of his informants amongst the local fishermen who claimed that large cargo ships, off the island's coast, had been sighted more frequently dumping some cargo in the sea supposedly to ease their loads, economize on fuel, and gain speed en route to their final destination. "What cargo," I inquired? "What route? Hell, what ships?" Chassengill asked me if I spoke Arabic and I replied in the affirmative. He must have suspected, judging from my name. We jumped into his military vehicle, and drove off to town to meet some of the fishermen, whom I was allowed, thanks to Chassengill, to interview at will and in their native language.

We arrived in the downtown area and headed straight to the fish market. Haythem Bakki was the local governor and the overseer of all villagers, inhabitants, and fishermen. We went to see him first. He approached us and exchanged few pleasantries with Chassengill. Then turning to me, he said in Arabic that ships were coming from the east, probably the Red Sea, loaded with bags of heavy salt. They'd gained the habit of late of stopping along the island's coast on their way to Singapore and dumping some of their excess cargo in the open sea. However, never before were such quantities of salt dumped, which, this time around, must have caused the ecological disaster. And how would he know all of that, I politely inquired? He replied that the fishermen had often recuperated some of the bags right after they were dumped. Salt usually floats to the surface (Archimedes would agree; how about you, my physics-ignorant readers?). Tight bags keep their bounce for a short while, just in time for the fishermen to pick them up. Did he or anyone else have any samples of the salt? I asked. No chance, said Bakki. What was left of it was either used or sold. That was about the most I could get out of him. I thanked him and headed back empty-handed (and empty-headed) to our military vehicle.

Chassengill drove off slowly in the narrow alley of the bazaar when suddenly we heard a voice from behind. A boy was shouting in Arabic for us to stop. I signaled to Chassengill to stop the Jeep and waited for the boy. He arrived after a minute or two, out of breath and carrying some folded piece of cloth in his hand. He looked me in the eyes and said: "Min Sheik Haythem" (which translates: From Haythem, the sheik). I took the cloth and unfolded it. My surprise was visible and I stayed speechless for few seconds. It was a bag, all right--one that had been picked up by the fishermen from the offloading ships, and to top it all, it had the Philadelphia Mines insignia written all over it. The potash trail was finally revealed. This hollow bag was my Rosetta Stone (no, you illiterate, no relation to Rolling Stone).

All that I am about to tell you now did not come to my mind at once, I must confess, but it got reconstructed piece by piece on my way back to London to face Sacks. My theory was simple. The potash was bought from the Dead Sea brims and hauled by cargo ships to Asia. However, en route, part of the shipments were slowly but surely offloaded onto the high sea to make room for another substance to replace it without raising any suspicions at the port of entry. All cargos are weighed at the ports of departure and of entry, so the balance had to be maintained. But what substance would that be? Well, the same that Brezwigt had stuffed up his nostrils (Cream powder. You wish! Heroin, you pazzis!) The potash was being wasted on plankton and turtles while loads of heroin were brought on board the ships by smaller speedboats, no doubt. Once in the Asian ports, the loads of the incoming ships would go undetected. They were part of an international commodity trade and, to boot, they had all the official documents and certificates asserting their origin: "Philadelphia Mines, Dead Sea, Jordan." The cargo ships kept sufficient quantities of potash on board to fool the authorities and carry on with the charade, which explains the inflationary price of potash due to its scarcity caused by the depletion of the world's stockpile.

Sacks heard my explanation with attention and much composure--no signs of surprise and no patronizing remarks, for a change. He was impressed by it, I could tell, but he concealed his state of mind. He simply nodded and left the room to make a few phone calls. I sat there, in his hotel suite, waiting for a validation of my theory or a termination of my association with Inter-Finance. I had cut a deal with the mob at a disadvantageous time, committed Inter-Finance to broker a trade with the Mabrouks not knowing whether they would go for it or not, breached the security of a US naval base, violated every rule of ethics by muzzling the media on Brezwigt's death, used with no prior authorization Selleck's contact with Chassengill, and kept Srocex in the dark for forty-eight hours. I could not think of a worse situation than the one I found myself in--and voluntarily, may I add. A designer's suicide belt. A tailor-made trap. (Okay, we got the point, said my inner literary critic.)

An hour later, Sacks re-emerged into the living room, calm but still chain smoking. His false grin turned into a genuine smile and I was instantly relieved. Apparently, after checking with the DEA and InterPol, my story was more than plausible. It was right on the money. Each agency had a piece of the puzzle, but none had been able to stitch them together. What sealed it for Sacks (and me) esd that the ships were all chartered by none other than Eastern Seaports, the corporate successor of Continental Traders. Got it?! Sacks had another piece of good news for me. The Mabrouks had accepted the mob's offer. I could bet on it, sort of.

I took leave from the Grand Marquis (aka Ramsay Sacks) and headed back to Rome. He even let me use his executive jet. I felt good about my achievements and he recognized my ascension inside the sacred temple of Inter-Finance. I did not want to face Wendy, who would have tons of questions about the ecological disaster in Oman. I had no clue--nor was I ready to reveal the true motives of my trip. So, I summoned Armando, dear old chap, and asked him to deliver a written message to her without revealing my whereabouts. Armando Domani was the most discreet of gentlemen, and one who rarely took credit (including the hard cash version of it) for his achievements. His contacts were unmatched, his actions punctuated with tactfulness, and his loyalty uncompromised. In the envelope, I wrote a tender good-bye note to Wendy, but with it, the falsified tax returns filed by the Azzurra chairman on behalf of his resorts in Miami and Puerto Rico, courtesy of Mark Wiesel, the ace US lawyer of Inter-Finance. Obviously, the moron was not only screwing the environment, but the IRS too. I hoped that this last piece of information would soothe Wendy's heartbreak by giving her the tools to annihilate the coral reef violator. That last note settled my debts in Rome with all.

ROTTEN TO THE CORE

We were having dinner at Soraya's parents' when the phone rang, and who was it for? Me, naturally! Nadia Gotryne knew my whereabouts and had passed the details to Sacks. I took the call, rather embarrassingly leaving my hosts at the table chatting about my future with my bride-to-be. *What timing*, I thought. Could that have been more inappropriate? Or was it? Sacks' voice was stern. I immediately knew something was wrong. "Hello," he said. "Wiesel was admitted this very morning to Mount Sinai Hospital in New York with a brain tumor." I was shaken by the terrible news and before I could answer, react, or even cough, Sacks continued, "I need you to be in London tomorrow for an urgent meeting and then you leave London to New York."

"Yes, sure, Ramsay--anything you say."

We finished dinner and I took leave of Soraya and my future in-laws. She knew something wasn't right. I told her all about Wiesel. She fully understood my predicament and insisted on accompanying me home to pack. I did not know how long I would be away, and settled on packing a light change of clothing. Wintertime in New York can be brutal, but I figured that while in the Big Apple, which I had visited only once before, I would swing by Brooks Brothers, my favorite NY clothing store. Soraya was saddened by the news of my departure. She always suspected that life with me was not going to be a walk in the park, but she had only started to realize how hard it would be: traveling at short notice, flying halfway across the globe, calling at odd hours, and showing up unannounced to leave again in the same style. She did not say a word, but I was reading the angst all over her face.

The trip to London was bumpy, with a lot of air turbulence. I consistently hated that, no matter how many times I had flown short or long distances. It just scared me every time around. Sacks' suite at the Dorchester was already filled with all the usual suspects: Gotryne, the lawyers and auditors, and other useless board members. However, Sacks was not home. He was at a closed briefing at the Exchequer. The chancellor had called him for an urgent meeting, so I was told. I tried to ask Nadia about the reason for my being summoned at such short notice, but apparently she had no clue. I believed her, since at this stage I was more involved in the internal affairs of Inter-Finance than she ever had been, and she somehow resented that.

Half an hour later, Sacks showed up, tired and in an abhorrent mood. He did not utter a word or make a gesture except to go to the bar and pour himself a drink. It was 11:00 a.m,! That was a bit early for happy hour, I figured. His butler walked in with a telegram from NY saying that the corporate counsel was in good health and that the doctors believed he had an operable tumor. That took a load off Sacks' mind, as he was tellingly pleased with this piece of good news.

Sacks needed to speak to me in private, so Gotryne and the rest of them had to evacuate the premises and make room for our egos. I doubted that both would fit in just one large suite. The City of London would have been a more appropriate venue, no doubt. "Wiesel could not have gotten ill at a worse time," Sacks said, in a somber tone. "We have grave issues at 15 Broad Street!"

Sacks embarked on a long tirade, which I will try to summarize in a chronological and understandable vernacular. From the old Wall Street partnerships, only few had survived the modern age. Some went out of business, while others went out of fashion. The era of "relationship-banking" ushered in by the likes of John Pierpont Morgan and Jacob Schiff, in the early 1900s, when private business passed from one generation of bankers to the next, was officially over. The present times were the age of super investment banks that could underwrite huge sums of money--and most importantly, "place" billions overnight with the new breed of investors: public pensions, mutual funds, commercial banks, endowments, and insurance companies.

One of Wall Street's most venerable partnerships that had survived the onslaught of financial supermarkets went by the name of Kuhn, Lipper & Katz. The firm was formed by Bavarian Jews–just like Goldman, and Warburg--who had emigrated to the Midwest at the turn of the century, and later moved their dry-goods business and commodities trading to the lower East Side of Manhattan. After World War I, the business of Kuhn, Lipper & Katz was run by second-generation émigrés who saw a much more lucrative business in stockbroking than brokering white cotton and black slaves. But the firm soon realized that brokerage alone was not sufficient to generate serious profits or to make one a wealthy and accepted individual in the high spheres of NY society, especially for a Jew. At such time, discounting trade bills and commercial papers became the firm's well-known craft amongst market operatives. Just before World War II, the business grew significantly into the debt market–a natural progression of its earlier model--to earn it a place on the US Treasury's list of official dealers. In nothing short of a transformation (forget assimilation), Kuhn, Lipper & Katz went from "bondage to bonds" in one generation!

Of the original founders, only the Katzes had survived. The post-war years, from the '50s to the '60s, saw the Baby Boomer generation entering the capital markets as individual investors, with IRAs and other forms of savings accounts. Kuhn, Lipper & Katz needed more money to keep up with the flow or face extinction. The capitalization of Wall Street firms was a merciless battle with "Bigger-Is-Better" as its hymn. The old behemoths of Wall Street--JP Morgan, Warburg, Kidder Peabody, and Rothschild-- had been challenged by a new breed of no less aggressive houses: Amex, Citigroup, Manny Hanny, Chemical, Bankers Trust, Merrill Lynch, and others.

In 1974 Otto Katz, the elder scion of the founding family, turned for counsel to an old family friend: Rabbi David Shreim. The rabbi was a wise man who lived in Brooklyn, and worshiped at the Magan Abraham synagogue to which Otto belonged. Rabbi Shreim was a Haredi. The majority of Haredi Jews were opposed to Zionism. This was chiefly due to the concern that secular nationalism would replace the Jewish faith and the observance of religion, and the view that it was forbidden for the Jews to reconstitute Jewish rule in the Land of Israel before the arrival of the Messiah. Although being himself an Ashkenazi Jew, Otto donated millions to Shreim for assisting Jewish émigrés from all over the world to properly settle in the safety of the US. Rabbi

Shreim, was originally Moroccan, from the city of Fez. His family was part of the Diaspora that had fled the Spanish Inquisition circa 1492, with some family members still living in Morocco to this day.

When Otto solicited his rabbi's counsel on how best to capitalize his merchant bank, without losing control of the business, the latter referred him to a man trusted by the King of Morocco: Jozef Azilou, a fellow Haredim. Azilou was briefed on the plight of Kuhn, Lipper & Katz, and as a result he arranged a meeting between Otto and Rutger Zarmat on New Year's Eve in 1975, in Marrakech, at a party hosted by the then ruling king, Mohammed V. Why was Zarmat chosen out of all people to be Otto's life-saving partner? Because Rutger's mother, Rachel, was Jozef Azilou's niece. (Need more explanations? Need a picture, maybe?) The rest is history. Zarmat agreed to capitalize Kuhn, Lipper & Katz, from the coffers of Inter-Finance, to the tune of $100 million via the issuance of perpetual preferred shares giving Inter-Finance veto right on decisive matters but no direct ownership or control, and leaving Otto in charge of day-to-day management. A holy marriage of financial convenience was born—a sort of sacred union between Nouveaux Bedouins and Old Hebrews. This investment in Kuhn, Lipper & Katz proved to be extremely prosperous, and by the same token, it gave Inter-Finance a foothold in the heart of Wall Street. Kuhn, Lipper & Katz' main offices were at 15 Broad Street (in the former glorious offices of John Pierpont Morgan), with branches in London and Hong Kong. It remained a force to be reckoned with in the fixed-income market, trading US Treasuries as well as illiquid Tsarist Russian bonds, Argentinian debt, commercial paper--and yes, more recently, high-yield (junk) bonds–the darlings of the day.

Now, I must fast-forward to the present time; otherwise some readers may fall asleep.

In London, today, Ramsay Sacks had an extensive meeting with the Chancellor of the Exchequer to discuss an ongoing investigation instigated by the NY attorney general. The investigation related to illegal practices at the weekly T-Bills auction, and Kuhn, Lipper & Katz was about to be named as a suspect. How does a treasury auction work, I dared ask? Sacks obliged with diplomacy and patience. "Each Treasury auction follows a similar three-part process. The auction is first announced through major newspapers and press releases. Bids are then taken and the securities are issued to the highest bidder. The announcement of a treasury auction usually takes place several days beforehand, but has been known to take place the day of the event. The Department of the Treasury publishes a multiple-month calendar that contains tentative auction dates. This calendar is published the first Wednesday of February, May, August and November. In the announcement, one learns the value of the securities the treasury is selling; the auction date; the maturity date; terms and conditions; eligible customers; bidding close times; and other useful information. Once the bidding period is open, financial institutions and individual investors may submit their bids. This is usually done through an authorized dealer such as Kuhn, Lipper & Katz. Following the auction, securities are delivered to the winning bidders. Winners may then hold on to that security until maturation, or sell before the security matures." (End of Treasury Auctions 101.)

For over eighty years Kuhn, Lipper & Katz had acted as an authorized dealer, with a scandal-free record, and now, all of a sudden it was facing a criminal investigation. This was disturbing, but the Chancellor of the Exchequer, according to Sacks, was not alarmed, since the firm operated only a relatively small branch in the City, but nonetheless "he was seriously concerned" --the politically correct phrase for alarmed!

Wiesel was, among his many duties, the Chief Counsel of Kuhn, Lipper & Katz. He formerly was the lead enforcement officer of the SEC. Wiesel was the "fixer" of the securities business. The SEC was not yet involved, but the office of the NY attorney general was no less aggressive or inquisitive. It was led by a self-obsessed zealot, a prosecutor by the name of Elbot Spinner, who relished his nickname as the "Sheriff of Wall Street" while coveting the governor's mansion in Albany.

What really worried Sacks was a potential leakage on Wall Street that Kuhn, Lipper & Katz was under a shadow of suspicion for improprieties in the treasury market. That would be sufficient to bring the entire house down. The firm dealt in billions of dollars and its liabilities would be claimed well beyond its balance sheet, reaching into the coffers of both the Katz family and Inter-Finance. With some confidence I advanced the theory of "limited liability," but Sacks was not a bit impressed with my legal argument. He had read law at Oxford and practiced with Freshfields in London, the Queen's Solicitors, before joining Inter-Finance. (s***t! I did not know that!). He politely–but with obvious irritation--explained to me that "piercing the corporate veil" was a common law principle that permitted to treat the rights or duties of a corporation as the rights or liabilities of its shareholders or directors, especially when fraud was involved. In criminal cases, a court would look beyond the "legal fiction" of a corporate structure into the reality of the business owners. In normal times, piercing the veil of Kuhn, Lipper & Katz would be next to impossible, but with allegations of illegal practices, and Elbot (idiot) Spinner in the driver's seat, it was guaranteed. (That was Corporate Law 101.)

With Wiesel incapacitated we had no legal counsel to counsel us--so to speak--and no means of stopping an ongoing investigation. Sacks spoke to Otto Katz, who, now in his mid-70s, ran no more the day-to-day operations of the firm, but kept a close watch over its affairs. He swore by the Talmud that none of the allegations were true. Sacks believed him, blindly, and I was to do the same with full faith and credit. Otto was family, and that was that! But who ran Kuhn, Lipper & Katz if it was not Otto? It was his son-in-law, Bruce Wolfosky, known to his close friends and foes as "Wolf," a moniker he earned years ago. Some say it was an endearing short version of his surname; others advanced a more somber tale. It went something like this: "Bruce had worked for seven years at Kuhn, Lipper & Katz before he caught Otto's eye, and before he got caught in Otto's daughter web, Kate. At the time, Kuhn, Lipper & Katz was not the first port of call for US Blue Chips seeking to issue bonds or other financial instruments. One CEO of such venerable company (Westinghouse) and of said creed (WASP) found himself in a bin. His company's excessive leverage had led to a downgrading by the major rating agencies. Raising additional equity was an option, but it would have been both costly and dilutive. Hoarding more conventional debt onto the balance sheet was not recommended, especially given the conservative bankers that Westinghouse had (Morgan Guarantee Trust, and Chase Manhattan). The CEO had no other financiers to turn to for advice.

It happened that his son was Bruce's classmate at Columbia University. He admired Bruce for his sharp intellect, and more for his sharper elbows. When the Westinghouse debt issue became a serious problem, the son recommended Kuhn, Lipper & Katz and, in particular, Bruce. He arranged for him to meet his father to discuss the matter over cigars and brandy. Bruce showed up prepared, and eager as ever to make an impression. He came, and listened to the detailed description of the capital structure of Westinghouse, asked questions, took notes, glanced at the financial data and intricate ratios, risks, provisos, etc. The works! He was convinced that Kuhn, Lipper & Katz could single-handedly raise $500 million in the form of convertible bonds for Westinghouse from Japanese and Arab investors, at attractive conversion rates--all with the help of Zarmat, of course.

The CEO of Westinghouse was both impressed and desperate. He agreed to the terms and when the engagement letter for Kuhn, Lipper & Katz was ready for execution, Bruce dropped a bombshell. He insisted on the CEO signing the engagement letter with one drop of blood, drawn from his pinky. He could not ask for a pound of flesh, since this was not Venice (for those of you who did not in the past, or do not intend in the future to, read Shakespeare, now is a good time to go to sleep). Bruce only wanted the Gentile to shed his blood for the Jew, in exchange for this elaborate financing scheme. It was Shylock's revenge, in addition to winning one of the largest blue chip accounts to the present day. This epic episode did not go unnoticed by Otto, who after this incident treated Bruce as family and elevated him into the firm's corporate hierarchy. Kate, Otto's daughter, met Bruce at several dinner parties hosted by her father and at outings in the Hamptons. When she got wind of the Westinghouse incident, Kate was rather amused and coined the nickname "Wolf" to describe the dark side of his personality. At the end the "Wolf" got his Little Riding Red Hood. "He had his Kate and ate her too."

Otto and Bruce were waiting for me in NY to bring them words of advice from Sacks. We met--of all places--in Wiesel's visitors' room at Mount Sinai Hospital. Loyalty until the last breath was the ethos by which Wiesel lived, and sadly died (a few months later). They all–except Wiesel--were a bit surprised by my young age, but kept a polite face. My closeness to Sacks and my position at Inter-Finance prevented them from making any offhand remarks. I listened to every detail. Nothing, according Kuhn, Lipper & Katz, justified such baseless claims asserted by the attorney general. As I quickly moved away from the legal technicalities they started listening to me, for a change. What could be the motivation of Spinner? Did the other blue chip investment banks had anything to do with it? What would they gain from the demise of Kuhn, Lipper & Katz? Had the firm's principals irked any politician, judge, mobster, or other powerful character, whether intentionally or not? Had they dealt with any shady character lately? They categorically denied any wrongdoing and dismissed all of my hypotheses. I had my doubts. We agreed on an action plan. Wiesel would massage a few of Spinner's office aides whom he knew personally. Apparently, we had a mole in his office who agreed to keep us alert of any developments. Otto agreed to work the grapevine of the investment banking community to monitor any newsworthy chatter. Bruce, who actually looked like a "Wolf," would continue to run a tight ship while keeping a close eye on employees and customers for any trail of improprieties. And I would be the "free neutron," looking in all the odd places and wrong directions, searching for the right answers.

We parted ways and I headed to the St Regis Hotel to catch up on some sleep. After few hours of rest, still with jet lag, I hurried down to the bar to experience the "original drink." According to an urban legend, a bartender from the St. Regis Hotel in NY, Fernand Petiot, invented the Red Snapper, which is a classy name for Bloody Mary, at the St. Regis in 1934. There is no horseradish in the original recipe! The bar was filled with ad executives from nearby Madison Avenue, loud bankers and gesticulating lawyers who had moved to midtown, and some tourists (from Iowa, I presume) wearing typical farmer's ties ornate with space ships. I was getting bored at the St. Regis and decided to take a stroll down 5th Avenue. It was around 11:30 p.m. It turned out to be the best hour to walk in mid-town Manhattan, with fewer cars, and a perfect time for window-shopping.

I passed St. Patrick's Cathedral, and crossed over to the Rockefeller Center toward the ice skating rink. The night was cold, and the smell of roasting chestnuts filled the air. I enjoyed the scenery for a while, headed back to the hotel, and crashed for a long night's sleep. I am easily awakened by noise in the night, but in NY even police sirens did not make a dent in my slumber. In some places some familiar noises become part of one's natural habitat, like the calls to prayer in Riyadh, or the loud salsa music in Buenos Aires. In NY it was the hustle and bustle of this gigantic metropolis that permeated your ears and became sort of an urban lullaby. Just because the city doesn't sleep, that does not mean you shouldn't.

The morning schedule was light and unencumbered with meetings or interviews. I made it to Central Park, and sat on a bench for a while. Unlike Paris, or London, on a business day NY is not filled with idiotic tourists disembarking from buses on a New World discovery. In NY you either work on Wall Street (lawyers, bankers, accountants, ad people, aspiring actresses, models, news anchors, etc.) or you are working the street (cops, politicians, mobsters, whores, pimps, union leaders, homeless). So if you have some free time in NY, you are sure to be left alone, almost lone-some. That's what I liked about this city of millions, where you could find a unique spot, and claim it as your own. They called it a melting pot, but I did not see anyone melting with anyone else--it was like a cultural quilt with each color, creed, religion, and race living next to each other...not with each other. Yet, the sum total was a magnificent formula for modern day life: "Tribes in Rags." Some Armani-made and some hand-me-down chiffons! You could choose the color of your rags since you could not choose the color of your skin. But the only color that really mattered was that of the greenback. Nowhere else in the world did the power of the $ manifest itself more than in NY. Everything in this town swirled around money: the bankers worshiped it, the investors valued it, the shoppers counted it, the tourists disposed of it, and the mobsters racketeered it. I decided to take it easy (as if I hadn't been so far?) and agreed to meet with a bunch of friends who were studying at NYU. A good pal of mine, Sam Gath, was enrolled in the MBA program over there. He threw the meanest parties with the most beautiful creatures (of the female gender, thank you), and served the best cocktail drinks.

In the meantime, "Wolf" called to check on me. I told him that I was on the trail and would call him as soon as I had some news. He in turn, informed me that because of Wiesel, that the investigation by the attorney general was being conducted at the behest of the US Treasury Department, and that it went all the way to the top. It was not just an auction impropriety...it was more serious than that. On that note, I snapped into action, headed toward the shower, and spent a whole hour bathing and pampering myself in anticipation of Sam's party. Sam's loft was located on Bleeker Street. It was huge and filled with a mixture of four geeks, two cool students, one certified junkie, sixteen wannabe models, and a good many guys and dolls, with the wonderful aroma of marijuana filling the room. Sam was at his best. He introduced me around to everyone as his "closest friend."

While catching up on old times with Sam, and mingling with the crowd, my eyes caught a glimpse of a girl sitting by the staircase reading some magazine. After few minutes of hesitation, I went across the room and introduced myself in the most idiotic manner: "Hi, am Sam's friend." She gave me the "so what?" look and we both laughed at my most unimpressive introduction. So I asked to be given a second chance to introduce myself: "Hi, Sam is my friend," and that second time around caused another roar. I could not get it right. The girl in front of me was breathtaking: a simple beauty with auburn hair, creamy skin, and dark- blue eyes. I was unable to focus or even pretend to be charming. I was like a kid in a chocolate factory staring at a caramel fountain and gasping.

The nymph took the initiative. "My name is Susan Otis-Warren, and I don't know who Sam is," she replied with a smile and a pronounced Bostonian accent. I had tried to introduce myself twice to a WASP snob hoping that by dropping Sam's name, I would get better acquainted, except that she did not know or cared who Sam was. Now that we were properly introduced, I sat next to her on the staircase and asked about her reading. She was immersed in a pamphlet written around 1775 by Thomas Paine, who according to Susan, was the man who inspired the Declaration of Independence. At this very moment, assembling my poor background on American history, I ventured to say that it was a well-established fact that Jefferson inspired and partly wrote that Declaration. "How typical of ignoramus foreigners," she replied. "You also think that the *Mayflower* was the first ship to land on these shores and that it was Columbus who discovered America!"

I was taken aback by this frontal assault on my exposed flank of poor American history. But before I had the chance to answer, the WASP-girl renewed her verbal attack, but it was less mortal than the first blow, I must admit. Sternly and with an air that exuded intellectual superiority, she explained to me who Thomas Paine was, the books he had authored, the pamphlets he wrote to inspire and warm the hearts of soldiers on the eve of decisive battles against the British, while fighting alongside the formidable General Washington. Jefferson was, in her own words, "A mixture of an aristocratic rebel and a weekend warrior," whilst Thomas Paine was the genuine product. The real McCoy! As for the first ship that landed on "these shores," as the broad insisted, it was the *Arabella*, and that on the 27th of May 1671. Her great-great grandfather was on that ship along with a host of Scottish families who crossed the Atlantic with their paintings on the upper deck, and their servants in the lower decks nestled against 1000 gallons of wine. Not the wretched of the world or the poor and huddled masses that arrived on the much-advertised *Mayflower*.

No longer willing to take it on the chin, I retorted, "Thanks to modern technology, I arrived two days earlier to glorious NY City--not to some forgotten Plymouth Rock--on a BA flight, in first class, with champagne flowing, and with no huddled masses in sight. A much less dramatic entry than your great-great grandfather," I conceded, "but more hygienic, and surely faster."

She liked my spirited reply and the cynicism in my remarks. We made peace and reached for drinks. We talked about various subjects that night and by midnight, the party was slowing down and we decided with Sam to head to Nell's, a trendy jazz bar in Greenwich Village.

Susan hailed a cab and offered me a lift. I was delighted, since I had no car and no clue where we were heading. We entered the bar. Sam had already arrived. He was sitting in a dimly lit alcove filled with some of the party's beautiful invitees (or more precisely, the delightful leftovers). We joined them--the music was swell, and drinks were full. I learned that Sam was a friend of Clarissa, Susan's roommate at Harvard, who tonight, apart from visiting NY, happened to be visiting his neck, chest, and lower back. I asked Sam discreetly who Susan was. He only hinted that she was old money, young body, and a mature mind. Go figure how to deal with this complex combination of qualities. We listened to good jazz being played, had few more drinks, and then, when I'd had enough, I took my leave around 1:00 a.m. Susan was somewhat disappointed that I had to leave; and we agreed to meet for lunch the very next day.

Arriving at the hotel, I had a message from Sacks. I called him back and he filled me in on the latest developments. The US Treasury was not after some insider trading case, as confirmed by Wiesel's informant. He asked me in a subtle tone, not to neglect looking beyond white-collar criminal circles. Did he suspect something more sinister? I went to sleep with my eyes wide open. If it were not securities violations that the US Treasury was after, what then could it be? I could not sleep properly. I woke up around 5:00 a.m. and headed toward Grand Central Station, the world's largest "human mill" where millions of travelers swirled through, going to work, coming from it, doing a job, faking it, telling, selling, eating, reading, scheming, and schlepping, in all possible directions. It also had the advantage of having the only combined bagel shop and newsstand open at this early-morning hour. Hurriedly, I reached into my pocket to pay the man at the counter and realized that I only had $100 bills. The guy looked at me with a grin on his face, and jokingly said, "Only tourists and drug dealers carry the Franklins." I looked stupefied and we both laughed about it. He gave me a bunch of single dollars in exchange so I could buy stuff without suspicion. As it turned out, the "George Washington" (the face on the $1 note) was the most mundane currency in the financial capital of the world!

The *Wall Street Journal*'s headlines were all about skyrocketing oil prices and the dependency of Western economies on OPEC producers. That topic gripped the financial markets and tormented economists both great (if any) and not so great (they're many). Oil producers did not produce hard or consumable goods. Goods–from cars to computers--were exported by non-oil-producing nations. Thus, a natural "barter" was established between those who sold the oil and those who manufactured the goods. When oil prices went up, manufactured goods became dear. However, when oil prices went down, the prices for goods did not necessarily follow. The oil producers felt constantly cheated and resorted to cartel-like pricing. The "barter" balance was seriously tilted.

Walking away, I was still reflecting on the sordid remark of the shopkeeper at Grand Central Station. The $1 bill was less-suspicious than the $100 bill in terms of exchange. A $1 aroused no concerns. So how did criminal enterprises that generated millions of $100 bills move their cash unhindered? There must be some other means than buying diamonds, or stuffing your mattress with cash. Money-laundering schemes of all shades were extremely difficult in the US, not because of the FBI's vigilance, but because of the zealotry of the IRS. It was the tax men that got Al Capone, not J. Edgar Hoover's G-Men. With credit cards and cashless transactions on the rise, even the $1 bill could soon become obsolete. It was a simple recycling dilemma. As in waste management, piles of cash (like trash) generated from an unlawful activity could not be simply hauled (moved across borders), or easily landfilled (in your mattress), or just sorted out (exchanged from large bills into small ones), and surely they could not be incinerated! Assuming the amounts would be in the millions, a solution had to be found. Money would have to be recycled from a "specific product"--that is, cash-- into a "generic product"--that is, cash-like.

What would turn specific money into generic money? I had not the faintest idea. I rushed downtown to see Wolf, during the early trading hours, and laid out my own "recycling" theory: the workings of the T-Bill auction were, I ventured, not the true subject of the investigation. Any illegal activity associated with T-Bills had to be linked to the recycling of cash. Laundering was easy, since TBs were issued in "bearer" form and hence, could not be traced. T-Bills could be deposited, held, or cashed at any bank without arousing the slightest suspicion. In fact $100 m in US T-Bills were easier to transport and cash than a fistful of $100 bills. But where did my hypothesis fail, according to Wolf? He explained that T-Bills were purchased via proper banking channels through firms like Kuhn, Lipper & Katz. That meant that the clients were known and the traceable or "clean" money was already in the system, thus, hardly in need of laundering. But I felt the roots of this plot to be deeper and much more convoluted than we thought. I had no means to provide any credible support for my allegations, but my heart was telling my mind to shut up, and it did…similar to love affairs…speaking of which, I sped to midtown for my luncheon meeting with Susan before she returned to Cambridge.

We met at Gino's, a lovely restaurant situated on Lexington Avenue not far away from Bloomingdale's. The joint was owned by the waiters, which gave them the right to be rude, and to move at their own pace. The lunch was delightful and Susan's company was as interesting as ever. She wanted to know all about me, including my daytime occupation, my travels, my worldviews, my hobbies. I just wanted to know more about her plans for the coming seventy-two hours. That was the width of my horizon. She was graduating in the spring, and decided to go work for a prestigious political publication called *Foreign Affairs*, as a young intern. I admired her lack of materialism. She must be either a saint or loaded with money, I said to myself. I detected no signs of holiness in Susan so I assumed her "Dad was rich and her Mom was good lookin'."

We had agreed to meet in Boston in a week's time. When it came to settle the bill, I tipped the waiter with a load of $1 bills, which brought an inquisitive look to Susan's face. To quell her surprise at seeing me carrying all single dollars, I used a topic close to her heart: American history, by telling her how much I admired Ben Franklin but could not use his $100 bills. She laughed and as we walked out of the door, she whispered in my ear: "You've got the wrong man!" I stopped and begged to have some clarifications to her remark. Did she mean Ben Franklin that I liked was not a great American?

"No, no, no," she replied, "you've got it all wrong, Ben Franklin is all right, but it should have been someone else's face on the $100 bill."

"What do you mean?" I said, innocently.

Susan, looking me straight in the eyes and holding my hand, started talking with a nervous tone. She politely derided me as usual for being an ignoramus who believed that Benjamin Franklin was anything but an overweight, shabbily dressed old man who tinkered with lightning rods whenever the weather permitted, pinched ladies' bottoms whenever the occasion presented itself, drank endless quantities of French wine, and soaked his body for hours in hot tubs every other day. All this was taking place during the American Revolution while Silas Deane, a Yale-educated lawyer, a successful Hartford merchant and an elected representative of Connecticut to the Continental Congress, was the real man, working tirelessly to convince the French monarchy to side with the young, rebellious colonies, arranging the smuggling of supplies and ammunitions into America in spite of the iron-clad British blockade, drafting the first and final versions of the Commerce Treaty at Versailles and being received as one of the three American commissioners to the Court of Louis XVI.

"Silas who?" I said.

Susan was not one bit impressed by what seemed an insolent query. "Your poor education is in want of serious enrichment," she said, in an imperial tone. "Things are not what they seem, you know."

Silas Dean, she went on was, behind the first victory against the British "redcoats." At the outset of the American Revolution a small company of British soldiers still manned Fort Ticonderoga, which was previously known as Fort Carillon, built by the French military between 1755 and 1759. On May 10, 1775, Ethan Allen,

Benedict Arnold, and the Green Mountain Boys--supported and financed by Silas Deane--crossed Lake Champlain from Vermont, and at dawn surprised and captured the sleeping garrison. This was the first American victory of the Revolutionary War.

She did not stop here. Deane had further contributed the cannons that defeated the king's army in Saratoga, and still, in his final hour, died in poverty, disgrace, and anonymity with no cannon salute at his burial, leaving debts, an infirm son, and a good name in want of vindication. At this junction, Susan was shaking and in tears and I stood there like a buffoon not knowing what to say or do. It was an awkward moment for both of us. She was breathless and I was baffled. She realized she needed to give me a bit more background about this story. We walked in silence toward Central Park and I wanted her to pick the time and place to spill the beans. We were approaching the Boathouse when she turned and faced me again, with sad eyes and trembling lips.

"Please forgive me, I get emotional all the times. Silas Dean was my mother's ancestor, and we have lived with this infamy for almost two centuries."

Apparently, Silas Deane was discredited, all his achievements attributed to someone else, his dues and expenses unpaid by Congress, and his name never officially recognized as one of the Founding Fathers. He ended up an obscure man who lived a public life and died in shame. This was the story told from one generation to the next in Susan's family, and it obviously left a social scar that obviously was far from being healed. This was the reason behind Susan's obsession with American history and her almost fanatical habit of correcting anyone (foreigner and indigenous alike) for the slightest mistakes, or false recounts of the past.

I would never have guessed. She was majoring in American history at Harvard University because she found Yale, Silas Deane's alma mater, too restrictive in thought and too biased in favor of Silas' enemies--although Yale's library, according to Susan, kept on display an essay in Latin written by Silas for future generations to learn from. I felt sorry for her and did not know, how I--a total stranger, as she kept reminding me--could be of any help or a source of solace.

She was too frail to go anywhere, and in my gentlemanly manner (yes, I do have this streak in me) I proposed that she spend the afternoon at the St. Regis and use the remarkable spa facilities of the hotel, while I headed back to the office. At night we planned to go to dinner, after which she would be driven back--in a chauffeured limousine--to icy-cold Boston. Sacks had asked me to call him and I had forgotten all about it. While Susan was half-asleep on my sofa, I called Sacks, who had some breaking news. He informed me that Inter-Finance's private bank in Geneva--Banque Prive de Placement or BPP--had received an unannounced visit from the US Treasury. The agents asked whether a particular individual had an account with BPP. Typically, our Swiss bankers did not reply and took notes of the request. Sacks interpreted that as an early warning signal by the US authorities. They knew full well that Swiss banking secrecy could not be violated, but probably wanted to alert us about their intentions without specifying their motives. The individual whose account they sought was a Scottish fellow who had been properly screened by BPP when he applied for a safe deposit box. He was a general physician with a thriving practice in Edinburgh, a matter confirmed by internal security, headed by our very own Georges Selleck, who conducted a background check on Dr. Adam Mitts. I asked Sacks if we could send Selleck to check Mitts' safe deposit box under the pretense of a fire alarm that necessitated the moving of all boxes into a temporary room. That would not even alert the BPP employees, who had to be kept in the dark for the sake of ensuring the utmost secrecy of our proceedings. The false fire alarm would take minutes and Selleck, who happened to be in Geneva this week, would check the box and report back. By now, Susan was sound asleep, and I decided to take a shower.

I silently and smoothly sat next to her on the large sofa, and Susan welcomed my closeness with a groan that did not ring with displeasure. She turned and embraced me, as if holding on to an anchor, and we fondly kissed for a while. I was hypnotized by her bright eyes, silken skin, and gentle demeanor. We took our time to get acquainted before we became literally one in body and soul. This heavenly moment was interrupted by a knock and an envelope slipped under the door. I fetched the envelope, which had only one word written on a white paper: "Bingo!" and signed by Selleck. I rushed to the phone and contacted my favorite mercenary, who sounded cocky. He was on to something. The safe deposit box was stuffed with US T-Bills. Who had paid the Scottish physician in T-Bills? Not his patients, I guessed. Selleck was on a hot trail and on the next flight to Edinburgh with the intention of sequestering Dr. Mitts until he revealed the origins of some $107 million in US T-Bills neatly folded in his safe deposit box.

Dr. Mitts lived in a bourgeois suburb with all the trappings of middle class life: a black Mercedes and a silver Range Rover; a pedigreed Labrador, a snob Siamese cat and a canary; a large Georgian house (not a mansion), a non-naturally blonde wife, and three kids attending public school. The family members had flown to the Tyrol Mountains on a skiing trip, and left Dad back home to tend to some urgent business before catching up in few days. The good doctor did not know what he was inviting by staying behind. Selleck sneaked into the house at night with his band of ninjas and held the doctor incommunicado. This was a misnomer. In fact he was too much "communicado" with Selleck, but not with the rest of the world. Selleck rarely used any violence on humans. He had a preference for psychological torture, like burning the Range Rover with the Labrador in it, putting the pussycat in the microwave oven, or eating the canary in front of a completely frightened doctor. These were the appetizers on this long journey on the road to perdition. I will spare you and me the gruesome details that followed and that brought the man to his knees begging to tell the full story, or at least his version of it.

The doctor had been vacationing in Mexico two years ago in Cancun when a Mexican gentleman made him an attractive offer. He was to receive on a monthly basis a pouch stuffed with $10m to $12m in US T-bills, all in bearer form. He would keep the T-bills in a safe deposit box at the BPP —whose code he shared with the Mexican mystery man--while keeping 1% of the total amount. The commission fees of the good doctor were packed in regular brown envelopes along with the *New England Journal of Medicine* and delivered to his doorstep by the Royal Mail. How neat and simple. Too simple. This was no normal organized crime laundering, since the Mexican counterpart had perfectly legit US T-bills. What was the origin of all that money? Did he have a name for this Mexican fellow? After the massacre of his pets, the burning of his cars, the shredding of his rare books, and sleepless nights under a glaring light, the doctor cracked up and emptied his guts, literally. He had the a name of a company registered in Nantes, France that he could call in extreme circumstances only, to leave a voice mail. The company's name was Beaumarchais—

How cultured, I thought. The quintessential playwright of the 18th century who wrote *Eugenie* and *The Barber of Seville* was now part of a dodgy network of hot money racing back and forth across the Atlantic.

Armed with this information, Selleck contacted his buddies at the CIA and asked them to lean hard on the boys from the US Treasury to get them off our backs. He gave them the doctor for debriefing. He would be part of the NY attorney general's investigation in due time. The barter worked and the folks at Kuhn, Lipper & Katz breathed a long-awaited sigh of relief. We were now free to unearth the trail without any of the US hounds on our backs.

Susan felt better, and was well-rested. So I decided to come along and accompany her to the campus. That would give us time to chat in the car. I also had the advantage of using the car phone to keep in touch with the office. I called Wolf on the road and asked him to research all names of the firm's clients who bought US T-bills at a regular pattern of $10m to $12m per month. He begrudgingly agreed to my request. He felt insulted by my insinuation that a customer of the firm could have anything to do with a money laundering scheme. I had not told him about our Scottish discovery and decided to keep him out of the loop, for everyone's sake. As we approached Boston, Susan, who had been tucked under a blanket and wrapped around me, readied herself for arrival at the Harvard Yard. She combed her hair but not too neatly, adjusted her sweater but not too tightly, and put on some lipstick but not too glossy. A well-crafted negligée look. I noticed! That was the entire point.

As I was helping her get the bags out of the limo, the phone car rang and it was Wolf. He gave me the name of seventeen customers who more or less fitted the profile I was looking for. I asked Susan to take the names down since I had no pencil or paper on me, and she obliged with a smile. When she handed me back the paper, one name jumped out of the list: Figaro! (Well, my dear readers, let me put on my glasses, get my culture stick and whip you into some shape. Figaro is the stage name given by Rossini to his opera, which was based on *The Barber of Seville*). "What is it with Beaumarchais?" I murmured.

It was not too much of a murmur. since Susan heard me and asked, "What about Beaumarchais?"

I did not know what to say. I uttered some incomprehensible words about a business enigma that I was trying to solve, but did not find where Beaumarchais fitted. She smiled, and with her angelic voice asked again, "Does your enigma involve smuggling, intrigue, and paper money?"

Wow!! I was blown away. Was Susan a spy planted to check on me, was she a psychic, or my Cassandra? Susan, realizing my surprise, gently took my hand, walked me toward an empty bench, took a seat next to me, and spoke softly but with authority. She told me that Beaumarchais was not only a playwright but also a secret agent for the Court of France who, along with (guess who?) Silas Deane formed a company that would smuggle arms and ammunition from the port of Nantes (of all places!) to the East Coast of America in support of the Revolutionaries. They got paid in "Continental dollars" rather than in gold or silver. Coins were heavier than paper money and were prone to theft by the British Navy or pirates (same thing) patrolling the high seas.

This girl was sent from the heavens to rescue me. The connection was solid between the Scottish (petless) doctor, the Beaumarchais & Co. located in Nantes, and the last-mile link to Kuhn, Lipper & Katz via the Figaro account. Knowing the details of the Figaro account would lead me to the Promised Land. I took my leave of Susan, and caught the next flight to NY. Wolf met me at the airport and on him were all the details of the Figaro account. In fact, Figaro was a sub-account of Santa Fe Petroleum, the largest oil company in the US. What was a sub-account? Wolf hurriedly explained that Santa Fe Petroleum bought oil from Mexico, regularly, by the truckload. Figaro Inc. was the Mexican trading firm who sold the oil and got paid in commercial notes (some sort of IOU) issued by Santa Fe Petroleum. Figaro Inc. took the notes and deposited them with Kuhn, Lipper & Katz. In turn the firm bought—at a hefty commission—US T-bills (in bearer form usually) for Figaro Inc.'s account. Kuhn, Lipper & Katz then discounted the commercial notes of Santa Fe Petroleum, keeping another chunk of commission on hand. We were getting somewhere, but where to in reality? Santa Fe Petroleum was next to God on America's corporate altar. It was the largest public company, the biggest employer, and the richest contributor to both Democrats and Republicans. How could it be connected to a money-laundering scheme? What was the role of Figaro Inc? The complexity factor shot up by an additional ten notches. I snapped into action, called Sacks and asked him to arrange a meeting with all relevant parties: the boys from Langley, the US Treasury, Wolf, and me. We had to connect the dots--but did I have to do it all by myself?

The next morning, we flew by private jet (boy, I was forgetting what a normal passenger ticket looked like) to Washington DC and came to 15 Pennsylvania Avenue. Wolf and I arrived first at the US Treasury. The folks there seemed pleased with the progress of our own investigation and the discovery of the bearer bonds cache in Switzerland. The CIA field officer looked like a McDonald's manager, with his short-sleeved white shirt, a collection of colored pens tucked in his breast pocket, and a JCPenney tie (that cost a penny, I presume). He kept quiet in a laborious attempt to convince us of an analytical mind at work. A nice group of losers, so far, until a man from Santa Fe Petroleum showed up in an impeccable attire (custom-tailored suit, laced shoes, Hermès tie, silver cuff links), and behind him, like a little boy in the presence of his school principal, stood (the erstwhile fearless) Elbot Spinner. What was going on? What was this guy doing here, and accompanied by Spinner, to boot?! Wasn't Santa Fe Petroleum under suspicion of aiding and abetting in the fraudulent activities that we were about to unfold?

Bech Korril was his name, corporate agent was his profession. No other introductions were made or judged necessary. He was dispatched by the fat cats of Santa Fe to offer his full cooperation, as well as Spinner's commitment to stop the investigation when Korril would deem it necessary. Spinner, not Korril, stated on behalf of Korril, not Spinner, that Santa Fe had agreed to provide all required assistance to uncover the shenanigans that might have taken place through the "unauthorized use" of corporate assets. According to Elbot's preliminary findings—when did he have time to make them?--any illegal act perpetrated using the name or facilities of Santa Fe Petroleum was never condoned by the company, its management, or its shareholders. How corporate America worked with the US government would put to shame any alliance between Hitler and Stalin. Santa Fe Petroleum was part of America Inc. and thus above reproach. I could tell that Bech was yielding more power in that room than any other person, including the tasteless CIA officer, the bean counters from the US Treasury, and the shamefully ambitious attorney feneral. The Eerie gang was reassembled, but this time to protect the robber barons, not to bring them down. Bech stated that this matter was one of national security, and out-of-reach of the law enforcement agencies. The buck stopped here. Why? Well, let's see. Would the fact that all (not most) members of the Treasury and Intelligence Oversight Committees in the US Congress were on the payroll of Santa Fe Petroleum, help in elucidating this riddle? With Bech Korril in the room, I was in the presence of real, not nominal, power. The kind that needed no planes or tanks, and relied on no thugs or licensed killers.

I knew whom to deal with from that moment on. Bech asked me where we could speak quietly and away from prying eyes and ears. He spoke softly--almost condescendingly. He knew where he stood, but he also knew that there was a serious cock-up at Santa Fe, which needed proper cleansing. My theory was intriguing to him. I advanced the scenario of someone at Santa Fe colluding with Figaro Inc. in a scheme to siphon off monies that were too large to handle in cash. They needed to recycle them into US T-bills, export them to Switzerland wholesale, and then import them retail to the respective members of that criminal corpus. Figaro Inc. was one of the authorized oil traders of Santa Fe. "We must start with Figaro Inc. and go all the way up that chain and into the corporate corridors of Santa Fe," I said. Who deals with Figaro Inc. from Santa Fe's side? What types of trades occur weekly or monthly? Any change in volumes? Any inconsistencies or abnormalities in payments, receipts, quantities, or quality of the oil delivered?

Bech assured me of getting the right answers as long as I kept the matter out of the limelight. I wanted the hound dogs of Elbot permanently off Kuhn, Lipper & Katz's back and the investigation officially closed, with our name cleared without a blemish. I required the support of the CIA in Mexico with the infamous federales (police) to uncover some unpleasantness at Figaro Inc.--and something much more! "What more do you want?" said Bech. I wanted Silas Deane to be restored by Congress to his full status as one of the men who signed the Alliance between the young American Nation and France. I wanted Congress to recognize his efforts and restore him to his righteous place in the pantheon of the great Founding Fathers. And I wanted his debts to be paid in today's value and in US T-bills (not Congressional dollars!) to his descendants. I wanted all of this in writing, signed by the Justice Department, before noon tomorrow! Bech was baffled by my request, but promised to deliver. I told him that for keeping Santa Fe's name in the dark, I insisted on restoring glory to Silas Deane's reputation. Bech acquiesced and I caught the next plane to Mexico. Georges Selleck was waiting for me at the Mexico City airport. He was fully briefed and fully armed. We were looking for a criminal connection with Figaro Inc., whose headquarters were located in the downtown area. The genesis of this affair must lie somewhere with Figaro Inc., but where?

Georges had arranged an encounter with Don Carlos Salidas, a reputed underground figure in Mexico who ran city brothels and drugs across the borders. Don Carlos had been in serious troubles with the federal police, which was busting his chops for more kickbacks, threatening his many businesses. He was looking for an armistice with the federales. He also, conveniently, had some juicy info on Figaro Inc. We had the CIA arrange a meeting between the commissioner of the federales and Don Carlos, at one of his best brothels. While the don and the police commissioner were conferring, the madam who ran the brothel came over to invite me to a special suite, that Don Carlos insisted I visit. Now I have done many unsavory things in my life, cheating on my fiancée and running loose around the world, but using the facilities of a brothel was not on the agenda. The madam insisted that it was very important that I grace the suite with my presence, as prescribed by Don Carlos. I had no other choice, but decided to abstain from carnal knowledge under any circumstances. I conceded to be compliant with the don's wishes, but remained observant to my principles.

I walked into this suite and a girl was sitting on the armchair of a lavish sofa. Her name was Teresa, and she wanted to convey an important message. She had a story to tell and inquired whether I wanted to hear it as a lullaby in bed or as a lecture on the desk or as a chat on the sofa. I must admit that her choices were all appealing, just like her physique. Mexican women can be amongst the sexiest on the planet. The Amerindians with their dark hair and brown eyes straight from Mexico are especially good looking. "Yalla, make up your mind," said Teresa, who spoke a few words of Arabic with a funny accent. Her dad, as I learned, was of Lebanese origin. Her grandfather had migrated to Mexico many decades ago. The wave of Middle Easterners--which included Armenians, Syrians, and Lebanese--came to Mexico in the early twentieth century and settled mainly in Baja, California and Sinaloa. The Lebanese in particular have settled in the urban spots of Mexico City, Guadalajara, Monterey, and Puebla.

Teresa was one of their descendants--and to my chagrin, not a working girl! She in fact was an undercover agent working for the Mexican government. She had secretly agreed to this meeting courtesy of the CIA! Her overtures were designed to test me. She never had any intention to seduce me; rather, she was brought in to brief me.

Mosley Hunt, Sante Fe's chief procurement officer, was illegal-
ly buying millions of dollars' worth of black market oil from
a criminal enterprise in Mexico and smuggling it–using Figaro
Inc.'s trucks--across the border. The black-market-oil gang–
which is organized like a small army–tapped remote pipelines in
Mexico to divert insane amounts of oil into their own stockpiles
for resale. Oil is Mexico's chief source of foreign income, which
brings in about 40% of the GDP each year. It's a black market
that was costing both the Mexcian and US governments tens of
millions of dollars per day in lost profits and uncollected taxes,
respectively. Because so many people depended on the revenues-
-from poor truck drivers, to ultra- rich oil barons in Mexico, to
Houston executives--the trade was too deeply rooted to stop.

The drain on oil revenues was weakening the effort to stabilize oil
prices in the US. Every day an average of 10,000 tons of gasoline,
diesel, and crude oil were bought by Mosley Hunt in the normal
course of business for Santa Fe, and sold through its legitimate
network, but never registered in the company's books. Mosley
Hunt bought it from an army of smugglers, who then loaded it
onto trucks, ships, and trains and headed into all the American
cities where Santa Fe Petroleum had gas stations, storage, and
distribution outlets. That oil outflow was enough to fill 325
trucks, or about 10 percent of Mexico's total output. It added up
to a loss of $1,250,000 a day, money that was robbed blind from
the Mexican treasury. The smugglers' gang was controlled by the
infamous Mexican mobster Felipe Juarez, who in turn was in ca-
hoots with Jonas Argenta, the CEO of Figaro Inc. This illegal
smuggling of black gold netted $300K per day in hard American
greenbacks, which amounted to $12 million or so a month! The

same figure was placed in US T-bills in the safe deposit box of BPP in Geneva.

Refineries in the United States bought millions of dollars' worth of oil from Santa Fe Petroleum, siphoned from Mexican government pipelines and smuggled across the border. Mosley Hunt used false import documents, fabricated under Figaro Inc.'s statements, to smuggle loads of oil to refineries in the United States. But Mosley Hunt concealed his trade brilliantly. He did not sell only to the refineries, but to small and medium-sized oil trading companies and even to independently run gas stations. Small and medium-sized firms paid in cash for the oil.

Thanks to Santa Fe Petroleum, oil theft had become a valuable trade on both sides of the border, beating drug cartels. But the breadth of the smuggling operation was a troubling sign of the growing reach of cross-border organized crime at a scale never attempted before.

From there on, things went very fast. Mosley Hunt was apprehended in the afternoon of that day while playing golf at his favorite all-whites club. I later learned that he had graduated with a law degree from Yale where he had read the essay of Silas Deane, preserved in the university's library, and was very moved by the story and the disgrace that befell the man. Hence, the emulation of the smuggling network and the trail he left behind that led to his demise. Don Carlos, our friendly mobster, got a respite of ten years and a 20 percent cut for the local police force--some sort of a "widows and orphans" fund for the federales. Santa Fe's name was never mentioned in the press and the hound dogs of Spinner were off forever. Jonas Argenta, the CEO of Figaro Inc., was also arrested, but the vile mobster Juarez, the man who reportedly never slept before getting even with his enemies, remained as elusive as a ghost. He was reeling from the destruction we brought upon his trafficking empire and vowed revenge, according to Teresa's sources. The name of Silas Deane was finally going to be cleared by Congress and regain its position in the hall of fame of American history. I was so excited and eager to surprise Susan with this wonderful news.

I rushed back to Boston, to see Susan, the true sleuth of this mystery. I was surprised to see, at the main college gate, policemen, an ambulance with open back doors, and a large crowd. I had a really bad feeling about this. A Boston police officer told me that a student had been poisoned and was about to be taken to the hospital. After waiting several minutes behind the police cordon in the freezing cold, the paramedics appeared, pushing a stretcher on which lay none other than Susan. I inquired about the hospital's address and immediately jumped into a cab, destination Mass General. We heard no news for hours. Susan's parents arrived from Connecticut, pale and desperate-looking. I did not know them, and did not introduce myself either. What did I have to say? "Hi, I knew your daughter, she is the champion who uncovered the enigma of an oil trafficking scheme of gigantic proportions?" Should I tell them that she single-handedly restored respect to her family's name after two centuries and brought them a few million in current-day money without recognition or thank yous?

The doctor came out and coldly announced Susan's death. Her heart had stopped due to a poisonous substance she had in her blood. Not waiting for any family member to react, I asked what kind of poison it was, and he replied that it was extremely rare. It was an extraction of a lethal seed that native Indian tribes in Mexico used on hair-thin arrows to kill their prey and enemies. It was called curare. A tribesman would blow tiny arrows through a short cane and hit the neck of the target. The arrow would leave no bigger trace than a mosquito's bite, yet it was sufficient to kill you. Was it a coincidence that a Mexican-made poison was at play? Only if you believe in fairy tales and happy endings.

I sat in the hospital hall, holding my head and crying silently. The phone was ringing. It was Ramsay Sacks. I could not bring myself to answer. No one around me knew or cared who I was, or why I was there, sobbing.

Life was rotten, I felt, rotten to the core....

Lightning Source UK Ltd.
Milton Keynes UK
UKHW010639120321
380227UK00001B/56